N'COLA

NICOLA
MARIO AZZURRINO

First published in 2022
by Jenner and Son
LONDON
ENGLAND

www.marioazzurrino.com

Typeset by Hewer Text UK Ltd, Edinburgh
Printed and bound in Great Britain by Clays Ltd, Elcograf S.p.A.

A CIP record for this book is available from the British Library.

PB ISBN 978-1-8384727-0-2
EB ISBN 978-1-8384727-1-9

2 4 6 8 10 9 7 5 3 1

Cover Design by Mario Azzurrino and Sarah Medway

Thanks to Alessandra Testai, the Mossery girls, Sarah Medway, Julie Thompsett, and Stephen King.

Dedicated to my family.

PART ONE

PART ONE

I

Nicola walked fast, her feet only now and then punching footsteps through the snow. She wished she hadn't had to leave him there overnight. Animals could have scattered his relics for miles around.

She arrived at the clump of spruce trees, a mile or so from the cabin and worked out where he was. She dug down a little with her gloved hands and found him. Luckily, enough snow had made it through the thin canopy of trees and covered him. She had a quick look around. No one else was there. She couldn't see or hear anyone else. She couldn't *feel* anyone else. Nicola went through his pockets and took his wallet. She took his pistol and removed the light chamois holster, cutting it off with her knife. His body had stiffened and he had frozen. As she searched him, it felt as if she was running her hands over a mannequin. She found what she needed. The thin chip-like piece of metal. She grasped it tight in her gloved hand and shut her eyes hard and gasped a guttural, deep sigh of relief. Nicola felt the weight of the world fall from her shoulders, but only for the briefest moment.

The chip was the key to David Klober's empire. Nicola wished she had shown it to him as he died. Shown him that she held in her hands the destruction of his life's work.

Something pricked at Nicola's ears. She turned to look back towards the cabin. A convoy of eight snowmobiles headed up the track and stopped out the front of the cabin. Eight men dressed in black rode on the snowmobiles. Armed with submachine guns. Two of the men dismounted. They looked inside the cabin. One looked down at the tracks that led to the clump of spruce trees and then they all headed fast towards Nicola.

Nicola looked down at her tracks and then at the distant figures growing closer. She looked up at the straight, tall spruce tree nearest to her. It had no low branches and would be too difficult to climb. She searched the body again for any extra ammunition, but there was nothing more. Nicola checked the pistol. Loaded with ten rounds. Fired in the last few hours. The clump of spruce trees was thin. No low undergrowth. Surrounded by open ground that was too big to cross in time. At the edge of the open ground were vast forests and Nicola wished she could make a break for it, but it was futile. She resolved to stand behind the tree. She racked the pistol and stood poised as the rasp of the snowmobile engines neared. Nicola checked the chip she had taken from the body was secure and took deep breaths and she waited. The rasping engines grew louder. She could now hear the snow squelch under the snowmobiles. Nicola

4

waited till the time was right, and then she made the move she had planned. Nicola shut her eyes and concentrated hard on the positions of the snowmobiles. She couldn't be sure if she was right, but she was out of time, so Nicola acted.

She moved out into the open and positioned the gun in a two-handed grip. The eight snowmobiles were in a V formation. The leader noticed Nicola and increased his speed. He moved a little ahead of the others and Nicola waited until he was in range.

She steadied herself. She dared to close her eyes for the briefest of moments to concentrate her aim. The man out front leant to his left. He steered the snowmobile hard at her and Nicola squeezed the trigger and she hit him in his left cheek. He seemed unaware of his wound and continued towards her. She dived out of the way and the snowmobile smashed into the tree next to her.

The snowmobiles circled round and round, their only hindrance being the spruce trees. Nicola could move between the trees, but the trees were a little too far apart. She took aim at another rider and missed. She was feeling as if she was going to lose the fight. Her morale slipped and one rider tried to run into her. She squeezed a shot and hit him in the shoulder. He fell from the machine and it stopped. He stumbled to his feet, clutching his shoulder. Nicola fired again and hit him under his left eye. He didn't get up again. She backed up to the tree, using it as a shield and to cover her from behind. One rider dismounted and ran towards her drawing a pistol in one easy sweep and he fired at her. The round slammed into the trunk of the spruce tree. He got down on one knee and began a succession of rapid shots. Nicola had to dive out of the way. Another rider crashed into her and threw her face down into the snow. The force was hard. Her ears rang.

She stumbled up and squeezed her hand where a gun should be. But she had dropped the pistol, and even with a clear head she would have struggled to find it. Knocked down again. This time she couldn't get up, but she was conscious, and she heard the snowmobiles stop, their engines shut down. She heard the crunching footsteps of six men approach. Nicola focused on the stinging pain of the snow in her face. The blackness, her eyes shut hard and her face buried in the snow. She focused hard on her hearing, not too bothered by the pain. Nicola worked out the positions of the men approaching. They would not get the chip and they would not take her. Not today. Never.

2

'I told you it wasn't a good idea—I told you we should have waited until she woke up,' the man said. Standing and looking down at his boss, who sat behind a big mahogany desk.

'That's beside the point, Michael—they know where she went, and they have found her,' she said.

'There is something about her—and she thought we were her friends.'

The woman got up from her desk and Michael flinched a little. Though he stood a good six inches taller than the middle-aged woman.

'She doesn't care about sides—all she wants is revenge and killing Klober wasn't enough.'

Michael shrugged. A look of incomprehension on his face.

'She wants to destroy his empire,' she said.

Michael still looked like he didn't get it, so the woman continued.

'We want his empire—it's the most valuable thing in the world—and we don't know the extent of it. None of your boys searched her when you picked her up!'

7

Her voice rose and ended with a shout and the man backed away, trying to hide his fear.

He took his leave and left the office. The woman stood there, her eyes fixed on him, her arms straight by her sides and her fists clenched.

*　*　*

The men grabbed Nicola by the arms. They tore at her clothes. They didn't speak, but she knew they were after the chip. They were also after extra justice and wanted to take it the only way they knew how. Nicola knew the danger. Their blood was up. The chip wedged into her jeans pocket. One man tried to force his fingers into her pockets. Nicola brought up her knees to make it harder. Her feet were grabbed, a man took each leg and pinned her down. They pulled her arms up over her head. They found her knife and tossed it. Nicola shut her eyes and prepared for what was to come. She hoped she could focus on the moment to make the memory more bearable.

Nicola felt the tight grip on her wrists. Both men seemed to have similar strength, and she twisted her wrists. The men seemed to lose their grip a little. This surprised her. She rotated her left wrist more. She could feel that the man holding it didn't seem to have the strength to stop her. She could feel he was panicking. It seemed the other men were unaware of his fear. The other two men groped her, exposing her breasts to the freezing air. Nicola tipped her head forward to see one man undo his zip. The other queued behind him.

8

A fire started in the depths of her unconscious. An ancient inferno had been lit down a long, long tunnel into the depths of ancient time. Her eyes burnt with rage and seemed to burn every inch of skin. Her body felt hard. Unbreakable. Her skin felt armour plated.

She rotated her wrists and made circles with her hands. She grabbed the hands of the men pinning her down and squeezed with all her might. She felt their flesh give way and bones crush. The rage rushed through her and their screams were faint to her.

Nicola sat upright. Her vision sharper than she remembered it. She ignored the blows raining down on her and she snatched her feet free from the other two men. Everything seemed slow, as if Nicola could control time. These strange sensations distracted and confused her.

Nicola drew her knees back fast, leant back and kicked out, letting go of the men's wrists and came fast to her feet. The man undoing his zip was still fumbling. But he looked up in time for Nicola to slam her forehead into the bridge of his nose. She felt the nose crunch and then also his cheekbones separate. She couldn't be sure, but she felt as if her forehead had half buried into his face. She brought both fists forward, and with perfect symmetry, she punched forwards into his ribs. They shattered and tore his lungs to shreds. His body flew into the man behind him, knocking him down. Being number two in the queue had saved his life. For now.

The two men who had been holding her feet were scrambling upright. Nicola focused on the man to the right, as he had the best grip on his weapon. Nicola lunged at him and grabbed the submachine gun. She smashed it into his face. She turned the weapon and flicked the switch to full auto. She spun round with the trigger squeezed. In less than eight seconds, all the men were dead, and the magazine was empty.

Nicola sat down hard in the crimson snow. 'Fuck,' she said.

3

'I can't get them on the comms,' the radio operator said.

'Try again,' Michael said, knowing instinctively that it was fruitless. I told her, he thought to himself. I told her, but she doesn't listen. He walked back to the boss's office and rapped on the door.

* * *

Nicola took one of the submachine guns and a few clips and rode a snowmobile back down to the cabin. She looked around for anything that could prove useful, some food, a little cash. She had to leave a vehicle behind. It was too risky to drive anywhere, and it was probably tracked.

Nicola took one last look around. Made sure her clothes were decent enough and took the chip out of her pocket to look at it. The chip was simple. It was a small, hard, piece of metal, less than half an inch square. In fact, it was dead on one centimetre square. It was low tech, invulnerable to hacking. It had on it something that would give her the key to the empire she wanted to destroy. She didn't know if it was a list, a set of instructions, or some kind of cryptic clue. It looked a little different from before. It had been stripped from a thin protective cover.

She knew it was the only one of its kind and that the only other source of this information was in the brain of a dead man. She also knew of the other interested party. It was powerful. Had the means and the reach to get to her wherever she was in the world. Even beyond. They had pretended to be her friends. But now she was surplus to their requirements. Nicola thought this was a shame. She had wanted to make use of them. She wanted their resources and to find out how powerful they were and then decide if they were to be next on her list. In the last twenty-four hours, they had decided that for her. She headed into the forests of the Jura.

* * *

Michael left the room with a cut on his head. His investment in the firm was worth the indignity, he thought, though he was doubting this. He held a crisp, white handkerchief to his head and walked past the secretary, who tried not to look. With every step, Michael felt emasculated, and his doubts grew stronger. He walked through the long network of shabby corridors down into the server room. The noise of the fans was uncomfortable, almost deafening. The room, cooled by a series of air conditioners, was still hot.

Michelle stood in the shadows and looked around at a rack of servers. She was nervous. As always. Worried that their meetings would end in discovery. She breathed relief that it was Michael that came through the door. Relief turned into concern. She saw Michael clutching the handkerchief to his head and she rushed towards him. She almost tripped on a bundle of cables. They wrapped their arms around each other, and the handkerchief fell to the ground.

4

Nicola was getting cold and tired. She needed shelter and came to a wide open, snow covered meadow. The light was fading and she was hungry. She could see a light far in the distance. The light brought her a slight glimmer of hope. But her hope faded. The light was far away and the very sight of it let her body relax, taking away its drive to go on. She didn't know if there was going to be a warm welcome, or if it was even a home to anyone. Nicola's instincts drew her to the light and she pressed on.

By the time she was near enough to see the place, the sky was dark, and she shivered. She could see now that it was a cabin. It looked neat and lived in. She imagined a well-kept garden under the blanket of snow. Nicola stashed the gun and ammunition in the garden. She thought of spring flowers and the warmth of summer, and it warmed her. The light from the windows high-lighted the steam on her breath. She hesitated. A girl-like fear of impropriety held her fast for a beat. She went forward to the door and knocked on it. She could smell food cooking. A stew. She stood back a little from the door and waited. She could feel someone approach the door. There was a brief hesitation from inside and she almost felt like running away. But then she heard the scratch of a bolt and the door creaked wide open.

Before Nicola stood an old lady. She was upright and elegant. She had a beautiful look. Her bone structure framing her looks for eternity.

'There is no need for the shotgun,' Nicola said. She was hugging herself. Her nose red, she shivered.

This surprised the old lady. She held a shotgun, but hidden from Nicola behind the door.

The old lady looked at the woman before her and warmed to the shivering creature. She thought that the young woman reminded her of a younger self. She almost looked as if she could be her daughter. She let Nicola in.

*   *   *

Michael left the server room first and Michelle a couple of minutes later. They had been in there twenty minutes. Michael didn't look back and went straight to his office to work out what to do. He almost forced out of his mind his prior act.

Michelle went to the bathroom attached to her office and wept. She washed herself as best she could. She composed herself and sat at her desk. She cleared her mind and read her brief. All it had were a few grainy images of Nicola, captured from security cameras, and an estimate of her height, weight and age.

Michael had the same brief. He looked down at it and felt blood run from the cut on his head. He grabbed a

16

tissue to stem it and looked hard at the grainy images. He got up and went to a large bookcase stuffed with files and papers from the archive of David Klober. He scanned his eyes over them. Amongst them were ancient scrolls, and he took one. He rolled it out. It was Japanese. The scroll had lived a hard life. He ignored the drawings and text and noticed right away the tear in it. Something had been in it. Michael guessed it was the chip they needed and looked closer at the scroll to find some cryptic clue. But it made no sense to him, and he discarded it. He went to his computer and looked on a map and drew a radius around the spot where Nicola was last seen. He followed his instincts. Looked at the contours of the ground and, using nothing but a series of hunches, worked out exactly where she was.

5

Nicola sat by a warm ceramic stove. The chair was a hard wooden chair softened by cushions and was very comfortable. The house filled with the smell of stew and was warm and felt safe. Nicola warmed. She stretched her feet towards the stove. Her outer clothes and boots were drying on a rack near it. The old lady was in the kitchen and hadn't asked her anything. She had spoken little to Nicola. The old lady called her to a small table with two places set. Nicola picked up a spoon to eat. The old lady glared at her and folded her hands to make a silent prayer. Nicola watched her until she had finished praying and they both ate in silence.

The women sat opposite each other. Their bowls empty. The old lady poured them both a homemade peach schnapps.

'What is your name?' the old lady said.

'Nicola.'

'A man's name?' the old lady said.

'Not where I'm from.'

'You seem to be in trouble Nicola.'

Nicola leant back and swigged down the schnapps.

The old lady got up and cleared the bowls from the table. She moved like a younger woman. Nicola's eyes followed her across the room. The old lady glanced back at Nicola over her shoulder.

Something pricked at Nicola's ears. She got up and went to the window. There was nothing, and she saw nothing. Snow was falling.

'Everything okay?' the old lady said. The feeling died away.

'Everything's okay,' Nicola said. 'I'm sorry . . . I never asked your name.'

'Josephine.'

'Thank you, Josephine.'

Nicola got her clothes and boots off the drying rack and put them on.

'Going already?' Josephine said.

'I don't want to get you in trouble.'

'You're safe here,' Josephine looked out of the window. 'It's starting to snow, your tracks will be covered, you will be safe.'

Nicola bit on her lip, looked out of the window again and fought between instinct and logic. The snow was getting harder. It would be soft and difficult to get through. She was under dressed and even if she didn't freeze, she would be too cold to fight well.

'Okay,' Nicola said, but she kept her clothes and boots on. Josephine poured another schnapps and offered Nicola the chair by the fire. Josephine sat in a matching chair opposite. Nicola shut her eyes and ran things through her mind. She tried to make a mental map of where she was and where to go.

'Want to tell me about your troubles?' Josephine said. Nicola said nothing for a little while.

'It is a long story.'

'I have a long time to listen,' Josephine said and she leant back in her chair.

Nicola ran the past year through her head. She fell into a trance. The images tore through her and she felt physical pain from the memories. Then she thought back two years further and a tear rolled down her cheek. The feeling of the tear snapped her out of her trance, and she wiped the tear away with her sleeve. She opened her mouth to speak, but she couldn't. It frightened her.

'I know,' Josephine said. 'I know what it is like to have things you can't speak of.'

Josephine closed her eyes, and Nicola did the same. She pushed her fears deep and forced herself to rest. She began to fall asleep and as she did, her head spun and she could feel her eyes roll back. *Oh no.* She thought.

6

Nicola descended into a world of black dreams. The things she couldn't talk about tortured her. She saw the faces of those she had lost and those she had killed.

Josephine got up and went to Nicola. She pushed up her eyelids to see the white eyes rolled back. She straightened Nicola up and made sure her head was comfortable. She wrapped a scarf around Nicola's neck to catch the dribble, and she put an old blanket over her to preserve her body heat. The drug Josephine had given to Nicola made her cold. It put her in a state of suspended animation. It slowed her heart and her breathing. Nicola was all but dead. Josephine reached under the scarf to check her pulse. She sat back in the chair and looked at Nicola for a while. Josephine then got up again and put a small footstool under Nicola's feet. She removed Nicola's boots and felt her feet. They were cold. Josephine threw more logs in the stove. She sat back down again and stared at Nicola. Josephine fumbled a tiny crucifix attached to a necklace around her neck.

'In about half an hour you will warm up a little, but you won't be able to move.'

Nicola didn't hear her. She was trapped in a space of shadows. She imagined herself drowning in a deep, freezing sea, wrapped tight in heavy chains. Josephine continued to watch. She fumbled the crucifix around her neck and then stroked the paper-like skin of her throat. Her fingers trembled. She got up and made trembling steps towards Nicola again. She felt the hair on Nicola's head and dabbed the dribble on the scarf. She straightened Nicola's face and propped up her head. Josephine's heart raced and she could barely catch her breath. Her fingers trembled more and more. She took Nicola's hand, but it was still too cold. She sat back down again, shaking with impatience.

Nicola began to groan and move. Josephine worried. She should be out for hours. She got up again and went to the kitchen and counted the pills left in the bottle. The amount was correct. She had used the right dose. She turned back. Nicola was gone. The front door was ajar. The thunder of helicopter blades neared.

7

Nicola's boots were undone. She struggled through the snow. It was snowing heavily, but she couldn't hide the trench like tracks she made. She saw the helicopter. Its search light beamed down on the cottage. Nicola's head spun.

She was difficult to drug. When she was a girl, a nurse had told her she was a fast metaboliser. Bad news if you wanted pain relief. Now it had saved her for the second time in a week. She had to get on and move into cover and hope her tracks wouldn't give her away. She checked the submachine gun and counted the clips. It was an MP5, an older model. Well used, but well maintained. She racked it and switched it to single shot. When she could get somewhere safe and lit, she would strip it and check it properly. She laced her boots up. Snow had got down into them and her feet were cold and wet. The helicopter thundered. The light beamed around and then the helicopter hovered. She counted four people jump out. They went into the cottage. Nicola made her way up a steep bank towards the woodland. She knew they would see the trench she was making in the snow, and she knew they were going to come for her. Then it dawned on her foggy mind that they would have heat cameras. Nicola trudged as fast as she could to the tree line. Her lungs burned and her body tired rapidly. She reached the tree line in time to hear the pitch of the helicopter blades change. She looked back to see the helicopter rise again and rotate, sweeping the area. Nicola forced herself behind a tree, putting the tree between her and the helicopter. She heard the chopping blades near and then become thunderous.

Snow whipped up under the wake of the blades and Nicola fought the urge to run. She waited and listened. The helicopter hovered for a while and then she heard it peel away. She waited until the sound faded to nothing and then let out a deep gasp. She slid down the tree. She almost collapsed. She felt the cold and thought on the vast distances before her. She clutched the submachine gun and for a brief second considered her options. Then she heard the crunch of a footstep in the snow.

Nicola slowly pushed herself upright against the tree and readied herself. The sound came from the other side of the tree. She waited for the sound of movement. She wasn't sure where to locate it. She was still groggy and cold. She feared her senses would let her down. They already had. If she was sharp, she would have felt another presence. She held her breath. Her heart pounded.

'I won't hurt you.'

It was a male voice and it sounded sincere.

'I want to help you,' he said.

Nicola stayed silent.

'I'm Michael.'

Nicola stepped out from behind the tree and aimed the MP5 at Michael's left eye. Michael raised his hands.

'I'm unarmed,' he said.

Her eyes darted around and then fixed firmly on him. Michael kept eye contact with her. Nicola approached him, stared ever deeper into his eyes and then knocked him unconscious with the butt of the gun.

8

Michael woke in pitch darkness. He almost thought he was dead. His head pounded and then gradually he made out faint shadows and shapes.

'You can't have it.'

Michael jumped at the voice. His breath quivered. Dull acoustics made the voice frightening and intimate.

'Where am I?' he said.

'Safe. For now.'

'It wasn't my idea to turn on you. I've come to make amends.'

'Too late.'

'We can work together.'

Nicola gave out a sarcastic chuckle.

'We thought you were going to die.'

Anger swelled in her. She remembered waking from the hospital bed. Nice room. Private. She woke up confused. A healed wound on her right shoulder. The door was closing to the private room. Her bedside cupboard door was open. She went to get up, tangled with tubes, realising one was down her throat. She fell. A nurse ran in. Nicola got up again, went to the window

29

and could see a man in the carpark below. A black Mercedes picked him up, Swiss plates, Zurich. It drove away fast. She remembered the chip. She remembered everything, including the Swiss plates on the black Mercedes.

'You took what was mine,' she said.

'You wouldn't have got it if it wasn't for us.'

Nicola couldn't argue. He was right. Michael's eyes darted unseen in the blackness.

'Where are we?' he said again.

'Hidden, out of sight, even from thermal cameras.'

'I've called them off,' Michael said.

'For how long?'

'Forty-eight hours.'

'Then what?'

'They will find us.'

'Then you will die,' Nicola said.

Nicola thought back to the doctors trying to calm her. She remembered her screams. She remembered the black Mercedes with the Swiss plates drive out of the carpark and disappear.

'Why didn't you take it sooner?' she said.

'To build trust.'

Nicola laughed and Michael flinched unseen in the darkness.

'Got impatient did you?' she said.

Michael nodded before realising the futility of the gesture.

'I didn't get impatient . . . I'm not the boss,' he said.

Nicola thought of the fight ahead of her. It made her feel exhausted. She thought of the added strain of a war on two fronts. She thought about swallowing her pride, for now, at least.

'Your boss disagrees with you, Michael. Even if I trusted you, which I don't.'

'I can deal with her,' he said. Michael felt optimistic. A load lightened.

Nicola stayed silent a little while. Michael was unarmed. He was brave. The people he worked for were unassailable, invisible. Hidden in plain sight.

'There's something about you Nicola,' he said. Nicola snapped out of her thoughts.

'We need you,' he said.

Nicola had heard it all before.

Michael saw the shadow move towards him and he flinched. A hand grabbed the scruff of his coat and pulled him up.

'Follow me,' she said.

He fumbled after the shadow. It took form as the light brightened. They reached the mouth of a small limestone cave. The early morning light blinded both of them. Nicola's eyes adjusted faster than his. Sky and snow sparkled.

'What now? What about your boss?' Nicola said.

'Leave her to me. She thinks she's smarter than me, she always has.'

'What about the rest of your organisation?'

'They'll fall in line. They're corporate types, in it for the money.'

Michael's eyes adjusted. The woman before him had a wild beauty and wide open eyes.

It began to snow, the light instantly faded.

'I'm keeping it for now,' Nicola said. 'Keep your people away from me. Keep them away from me long enough for me to trust you.'

Nicola turned from him and walked up over the steep slope above the cave and into the forest.

Michael watched her walk away, then sat hard in the snow.

'Fuck,' he said.

*   *   *

Nicola made her way up to higher ground. She felt as if she was running out of lives. In the last year she had woken up on a hospital bed more often than most people do in a lifetime. She could have asked Michael for help. Some more clothes, money, documents, visas. But she didn't want to. She could cope.

She wondered why Michael hadn't asked her about why she wanted to kill Klober twice. Maybe they knew why, or maybe they didn't care. She had got to Klober all on her own. It had taken them years to get close and they still would have failed. Nicola felt for the chip in her pocket. It was there. She took it and looked at it. She held it close to her eye and could see a smooth border around the edge on both sides. Inside the border, the metal looked matt. Caused by whatever is etched on it, she thought. David Klober had something that was so important, he didn't want to risk it to memory. She put the chip deep in her pocket.

Nicola made it to a clearing high up and could see a town nearby.

* * *

Michael called in and let Michelle know he was ok. She was relieved. Keeping things from the boss was difficult. Keeping her fear about Michael's safety was harder.

'Did she miss me?' he said.

'She feels guilty about before, as usual,' Michelle said.

Michael said nothing. He knew the boss was incapable of guilt.

'Meet me,' she said.

Michael paused and thought. Michelle agonised in the silence.

'Okay. Where?' he said.

9

Nicola stripped the gun down to its individual components and scattered them. She kept the rounds a while longer and then scattered them too. She was underdressed. She had a little cash, enough for a coffee maybe. She was hungry, thirsty and freezing cold. She adjusted her clothes and smartened herself up as best she could. She put her hands in her pockets, kept her head down and walked along the greasy wet tarmac of the road into town.

She went into a small cafe and ordered coffee. That *was* all she had enough for. She sat by a window and looked out at the street. She ignored the cursory glances of the owner and the other customers. Most of the customers were dressed in warm coats, some were in ski gear. She hugged the coffee cup and sipped it. Nicola felt too conspicuous. She felt stupid. She finished her coffee and got up to leave, when a woman approached her and threw an envelope on the table. The woman walked away without a word and left the cafe.

Nicola looked down at the envelope and picked it up. Written on the front: *Don't be stubborn. Michael.* It had three thousand Swiss francs inside. Crisp, sky blue hundred-franc notes. Nicola had no choice but to spend it, and this made her feel as if they had trapped her.

* * *

They woke early and held each other. Michelle then got up and showered and dressed. Neither of them spoke. Michelle left the hotel, leaving Michael to stare up at the ceiling and think.

Michelle arrived back at the office. It was a small building, made out of an old townhouse on the outskirts of Paris. There were other businesses in the street, based out of similar houses. Her organisation chose this spot because it was inconspicuous. Hidden in plain sight. It had a few employees, held on a tight leash. Everyone strictly vetted. Michelle felt a knot of nausea as she approached the building. She always did, but no one else could tell. She pushed open the battered, creaking front door, nodded to the concierge and climbed the stairs. The boss appeared on the landing as she reached the top and Michelle looked her in the eye and smiled, though inside she felt like screaming.

'Come into my office,' the boss said and Michelle followed her.

She sat down and the boss took her place behind the big desk and looked hard at Michelle. Michelle looked back. There was silence. An attempt to intimidate. It worked, but Michelle didn't show it.

'Where have you been?' she said, leaning towards Michelle, her elbows on the desk.

'I met with Michael, he has some information.'

The boss paused a beat. Again, to intimidate. Michelle felt hot around her neck. She hoped she wouldn't visibly sweat.

'And?' the boss said.

'He knows where she is, he's handling it.'

The boss leant back. Said nothing and stared at Michelle.

'You know I have your best interests at heart,' she said.

Michelle nodded, only half believing her. She needed to believe her. The boss got up and walked around the desk. Michelle tried not to flinch as the woman gently teased a stray hair from Michelle's forehead. Both women said nothing for about half a minute before the boss broke the silence.

'You can go now,' she said and Michelle got up with as much dignity as she could and left the office. As the door shut behind her, Michelle took a deep breath. The sweat chilled her skin. She scuttled to her office. She had to sit. She hyperventilated a little, picked up her phone and sent a message to Michael. *She's onto us.*

* * *

Nicola was newly clothed and fed. She blended in now. Warm and looking like everyone else. She had found a small hotel and booked herself in for a couple of nights. She had no doubt about being watched and knew that they would contact her when they judged the time was right.

37

She sat at a small table by the window, looking down at the street below. She took the chip out of her pocket and placed it on the table. It looked like nothing. She bent over it to look as close as she could, but it was meaningless. She wondered if David had made a machine that could read it. One of a kind, found nowhere else. If that was so, then the chip was worthless. She pushed it about a little with her finger. It was like the soul of David Klober. Written on it were his deepest secrets. Nicola hated him. She had killed him. She had watched him die, but through this tiny piece of metal he lived. He mocked her still and she still felt raw and unsated. She took a napkin, laid it out on the table and wrapped the chip. She pushed the package into her side pocket. She could feel it tight against her thigh.

* * *

Michael looked down at his phone. *She's onto us.* He wasn't worried. He knew she wasn't and even if she was, the wheels were too far in motion. New leadership was long overdue, and in this organisation, the recruitment process was, you could say, informal. Nicola, this strange entity, that appeared from nowhere, happened on her watch. It doesn't matter who missed her, if there were operational errors. It happened on her watch and it was her fault. That is what bosses are for if nothing else. To lead by example, and to be made an example of.

10

Nicola woke and got out in the early morning air. It was fresh and crisp. A magical blanket of snow everywhere. Only a few people were out. She walked through canyons of ancient buildings and down towards the vast lake. She felt, for a moment, as if she was on holiday. She cast her eyes across to the distant shores of the lake. The mountains were hidden in mist, but you could feel their presence.

A man approached her and coughed. He looked a little embarrassed and tired. He handed Nicola an envelope, gave a shy, apologetic smile, nodded and then walked away. Nicola rolled her eyes and opened the envelope. It was a tourist map. A cafe was circled on the map and an arrow pointed to where Nicola stood. She made her way to the cafe. Her step no longer relaxed, tension building in her body with every step. She approached the cafe. It was closed, but Michael came to the door and opened it. Nicola went in and Michael shut and locked the door. They went out back to a table out of sight. There were two coffees ready on the table. They both sat.

'Sorry if you're hungry . . . kitchen's not open yet,' he said.

'I'm fine.'

Michael nervously tapped his knuckles on the table for a few seconds.

'You ready?' he said.

Nicola sighed and took the folded napkin out of her pocket and put it on the table. Michael reached out for it. Nicola put her hand on top of his. Michael looked down at her elegant hand. It was warm and he enjoyed the feel of her hand on his.

'We stay together,' she said and she lifted his hand off the napkin.

Michael gave a single nod.

'You know how to read this thing?' Nicola said.

'We have a pretty good idea. We think it just needs a good microscope.'

Nicola drained her coffee cup, stood up and put the napkin back in her pocket.

'Then let's go,' she said.

Michael stood up. He thought of excuses to delay her. Legitimate excuses, but he knew there was no arguing, so he finished his coffee, and they went out into the street.

'So where are we going?' Nicola said.

'A local university. I have a friend there.'

'You don't have your own labs?'

'We do, but we can't go there.'

Nicola thought about the infighting that must be going on in Michael's organisation and she wondered how it would interfere with her plans. But she had no choice but to trust him. She needed to make use of him.

If they can find out what's on the chip in the next hour or so, then that will be enough. Maybe she would be done with them by the end of the day.

They took a small bus to the outer limits of the town to a small university campus. Michael waved a pass at the gate and they walked into one of the older buildings. They were greeted by a tall, serious looking man. He shook Michael by the hand and then shook Nicola's hand. Nicola introduced herself.

'I'm Peter, an old friend of Michael's.'

They followed Peter up a flight of stairs to a cluttered lab, humming with various pieces of equipment. Students walked in and out, some said 'hello,' others seemed oblivious to any other person. The lab was old, built in the nineteen sixties. The benches were made from a dark wood, the tops were covered with temporary surfaces.

They squeezed through the clutter to a side room. A large microscope sat on a desk. It too looked old, but well kept, and perfectly functional.

'Can I have a look at it?' Peter said. Nicola put the napkin on the desk and opened it. Peter picked up the chip and Nicola felt an internal flinch. She couldn't bear the sight of someone else holding the chip.

Peter looked closely at the chip and using a pair of tweezers he put it on a small mount and placed it in the microscope. An image appeared on a monitor next to the microscope. The textured area of the chip was now visible as a series of parallel lines. Peter focused into the lines.

The image dived into the centre of the chip and the lines became clearer and sharper.

The lines divided into pits, triangular shaped. Like the negative image of tiny pyramids.

'I don't understand this,' Peter said.

Nicola looked hard at the image.

'They are all slightly different,' she said.

Peter and Michael leaned in at the screen.

'I see,' Michael said. The microscopic, negative impressions of pyramids were all asymmetrical. Each one seemed to be unique, and this was just a microscopic fragment of the chip.

'I have no idea what it means,' Peter said.

'Have you seen anything like this before?' Michael said.

'No, never,' and Peter leant back and shook his head.

Nicola felt angry. Her ears rang with the pressure of rage in her skull. She pictured David laughing. His arrogance. His presence. Had he really died? She felt he hadn't. He seemed stronger and more alive than he ever had been. She closed her eyes tight.

'Do they point to something?' she said.

'What?' Peter said.

'Do they point to a grid of letters or symbols?'

Michael and Peter looked again at the screen. Peter scanned around the image, zooming in and out.

'In theory you mean?' Michael said.

Nicola grabbed a sheet of paper and held out her hand for a pen. Peter felt around in his pockets and found a pencil. He gave it to Nicola, who snatched it and began to draw a grid on the paper. She filled in the boxes with letters. She hovered her finger above the grid of letters.

'The angle of each inverted triangle points to a letter,' she said.

'Or some other kind of symbol,' Peter said.

'Like what?' Michael said.

'I don't know! Hexadecimal maybe?'

Peter took the paper and pencil from Nicola and drew another grid. He wrote numbers and letters in the boxes.

'It could lead to another layer of encryption though,' Peter said.

The three of them were silent. Deep in thought.

'This is going to take ages,' Nicola said.

Peter chewed on the pencil and drummed his fingers on the table.

'I think I know a way of speeding things up,' Peter said.

He took the mount out of the microscope and handed it to Nicola.

He stood up and walked out of the room and they followed him back through the cluttered lab, along a corridor and into a newer wing of the building. They walked through the swing doors of a larger modern lab. Peter nodded to students and fumbled a bunch of keys. Peter came to a door with 'AFM' written on it. He looked at an indicator above the door to check that the room was free, and he unlocked it and went in. Nicola and Michael followed. On a table was a modern-looking microscope next to a computer and some kind of control unit.

'I can use this, at least I think I can,' Peter said.

'Another microscope?' Michael said.

'Different, more powerful, but maybe too powerful. I think I can get it to work if I can turn down the power.'

Peter fumbled in his pockets.

'I need to get my login for the machine.'

Peter left Michael and Nicola in the room and went out the door. It closed behind him.

'Who is Peter?' Nicola said.

'He's a technician.'

'Not a scientist?'

'No. He's practical,' Michael said.

'How do you know him?'

'He's a childhood friend.'

'He doesn't seem that friendly towards you.'

'He wanted to work for us. I blocked his application.'

'Why?'

'For his best interests.'

'Can you trust him?'

Michael nodded and sat in the chair. Nicola paced around and looked at the microscope.

'What is this thing?' she said.

'I have no idea.'

They were silent. The light in the room was harsh. There were no windows. Above the desk there was a shelf that had box files. Nicola took one and flicked through it, but it made no sense to her. It was full of technical jargon. The results of some experiment. Lists of setup protocols. She put the file back and sat on the desk. Michael watched her backside press

44

against the desk and admired the shape of her legs. He looked at her elegant fingers wrapped around the edge of the desk.

'How long does it take to go up that corridor and back again?' Nicola said.

Nicola reached into her pocket and took out the sample mount. It was empty.

A cold wave rushed over them and Michael jumped out of the chair. Nicola leapt from the desk and grabbed the door handle and pulled it. The door was locked. She rattled it and thumped, but it wouldn't give. Michael barged at it with his shoulder, but it wouldn't give. Nicola kicked. The door dented and Nicola and Michael alternated with kicks and shoulder barges. Eventually the door broke and they could force their way out. Two students stared at them, mouths open. They went back along the corridor, through the lab and into the room with the microscope. The chip was gone.

They went down to the reception area of the building. There was a concierge, and they asked him if he had seen Peter, but he hadn't. He had seen no one. They went outside the building, but life was normal. Peter was nowhere to be seen. Nicola glared at Michael, who said nothing. His head was whirring with panic and shame. He had been outmanoeuvred. The possibilities fired around in his brain. Did Peter work alone? Was the boss in it all along? He even thought of the possibility that it could have been Michelle. He thought of their forbidden love/hate trysts. Did she hate him more than love him? Nicola and Michael span around, back-to-back, taking in the immediate world around them, determined to see something that would help. They went to the guard at the entrance to the campus. He knew nothing, had seen no one. It was no good. The chip was gone. Again.

11

Nicola screamed into her cupped hands. She grabbed Michael.

'This better have nothing to do with you!' she said.

She knew it wasn't him though. She could see it in his eyes. Michael said nothing. His head still whirred. He felt as if he was going to vomit. Michael's phone buzzed. There was a message. It was from the boss. *I need to see you. Now.* Michael ran to a cluster of bushes and vomited. Nicola thought of what to do. Should she abandon Michael? Should she give up on the whole thing? Live with it? The second the thought entered her head, the thought of living with it, she knew that would be unbearable. She would rather die.

'I have to go,' Michael said.

'Where?'

'I've got to go. You need to hide. You need to go now.'

Michael walked away, half staggering. Nicola knew there was no point arguing with him. But she wasn't going to let him out of her sight. She held back and followed him. She watched him walk away and as he became more distant, she decided to run after him.

Michael flinched as she put her hand on his shoulder. He looked white and dark circles already surrounded his eyes.

'I'm coming with you. I have nowhere else to go,' she said.

Michael looked relieved. He didn't have the strength to argue. He felt as if he was plunging off a cliff. Nicola felt the same, but she drew every reserve she had to keep focused.

'I've been summoned,' Michael said.

'Where to?'

'Our HQ in Paris.'

'It's just as quick to drive there,' Nicola said.

She grabbed Michael by the arm.

'Sort out a hire car,' she said.

Michael looked on his phone and they walked down into town. He gradually calmed down. Nicola felt some pity towards him. Michael looked again at his phone and made a call. They both sat on a bench at the corner of two streets. Five minutes later a new Mercedes saloon pulled up and the driver handed over the keys and walked away.

'I'll drive,' Nicola said and Michael agreed.

Michael punched in the address. A small street in the Paris suburbs, not far from Versailles. They settled into the comfortable seats and the car purred into life. Nicola drove fast and they were soon across the border into France. Both felt heady as the adrenaline wore off. For the first hour they were silent.

12

The boss walked around the block with a tall, older, sombre man.

'I hope your house is in order,' he said.

'It is,' she said defensively.

'There are rumours,' he said.

'I have the chip,' she said. The man stopped walking, taking her by surprise. A smile cracked across his face and they resumed their walk.

'It would be easier if we could all meet together,' she said.

'You know that isn't possible.'

'I always feel out of the loop,' she said.

'We all feel out of the loop. It's how it was set up and this way, it is in all our interests, you know that.'

'Well, it's all in order. I will let you all know when I have the information. Good day.'

She walked back to the building alone, up the staircase and into her office. She called Michelle.

'I want to see you,' she said. Within a minute Michelle knocked on the door. She was called in and told to sit.

The boss sat and looked at Michelle, but the look was one of sadness. A look that Michelle was sure she had never seen before.

'What have you two done?' she said. Michelle gulped and squeezed her thighs together. Words failed to leave her lips. Her throat was bone dry.

'Get some water.'

Michelle got up and shaking she poured a glass of water, almost dropping both the glass and the jug.

She sat back down, pressed her knees together and drank from the glass, still shaking.

'Michael is on his way back, but I want to speak to you first, give me your phone.'

Michelle took her phone from her pocket and slid it across the desk. The older woman dropped it into a desk drawer, locking it.

'What have you done?' she said again. Her tone was becoming menacing, the pity in her voice giving way to rage.

Michelle began to feel weariness. For the first time in her life, she began to feel tired of feeling afraid.

'We've done everything we had to,' she said. The older woman drew back. She was shocked. She hadn't ever seen so much as a shade of defiance before.

'We did all we can for us, for the organisation, like you taught us, like you have always taught us,' Michelle continued. She took a risk. She pushed out of her mind her illicit meetings with Michael. She hoped this was beyond the older woman's comprehension.

'You both think you have what it takes to replace me?' the boss said.

Michelle frowned, putting a confused expression on her face. She shook her head and opened her mouth slightly to emphasise.

'I don't want anything to do with this anymore,' Michelle said.

'Does Michael feel the same?'

Michelle nodded. 'I think so,' she said.

The older woman burst into a rage. She stood and swept her arm across the desk, pushing its ornaments onto the floor. Michelle fell back off her chair in fright. The boss now stood over her, her fists clenched.

'I know what you've been up to. I know everything,' she growled. Michelle retched and slid away from her.

'Get out!' she pointed at the door and Michelle struggled to her feet and stumbled out of the office. She went to the bathroom and vomited. She went to check her phone, then remembered it was in the boss's desk. Another wave of panic and nausea broke over her. She thought of suicide.

13

'You know who has the chip, don't you?' Nicola said. Michael nodded.

'My company has it,' he said. Nicola knew this anyway. There could be no one else.

'And Peter?' she said.

Michael looked into his lap, screwed up his face and shook his head. Nicola turned her attention back to the road.

'Is it safe to go back there?' she said.

'No.'

'Then what are we doing?'

'It's not safe anywhere. They will be following us now. They see everything, you know this,' Michael said.

Nicola thought of the chances and possibilities. Either way, she would not give up. She knew she would rather die. She looked at the cars ahead and behind and wondered which of them were following her. They probably had trackers in the car she was in anyway.

'Why didn't you just let them take it?' she said.

'I just wanted to be right for once, to do the right thing. I have done so many bad things.'

Nicola said nothing and focused harder on the road. It didn't seem that five hours had passed as they approached the south-west outskirts of Paris.

Nicola followed the directions to the headquarters. She was now aware of two cars following them, unable to hide in the quieter streets. As they turned the corner Nicola felt great foreboding. Michael was silent and pale. The two cars following were making no attempt now to hide or hold back. They turned another corner into the final destination. Nicola had to slam on the brakes. Police tape stretched across the end of the street and a gendarme stood guard. Nicola and Michael got out of the car and looked down the street. The doors to an ambulance were closing and then the ambulance drove away, out the other end of the street. The cars following them also stopped. Two men got out of each and they looked confused, unable to respond. They ignored Michael and Nicola. They got back into their cars and turned around and drove away.

'What's going on?' Michael said to the gendarme.

'Do you have anything to do with this place?' the gendarme said.

Michael nodded and showed some identification. The gendarme spoke on his radio and soon a detective approached.

'Hello Michael,' he said and glanced at Nicola.

'Phillippe! What's happened?'

'Come with me, she with you?'

'Yes, she's fine.'

They followed Phillippe to the headquarters building. The gendarmerie heavily guarded the area.

Michael looked at the armed men and at Phillippe.

'You know you are far too important to be left alone to us humble policemen,' Phillippe said.

They entered the building. There were spots of blood in the doorway. Nicola didn't speak. She looked around at the humble building, wondering if the chip was here.

They went up the ornate staircase to the upper landing. The lights flickered, probably an indication of a silent alarm. None of the staff were there. There were fragments of broken porcelain on the floor. The boss's door was open. They followed Phillippe into the office. There was blood everywhere. Thick and congealing. The bittersweet, iron aroma of the blood filled the air. There was a shoe on the floor, lying in the blood. It was one of the boss's shoes.

Michael looked at Phillippe in horror, speechless.

'Your mother is dead, your sister killed her and then she killed herself.'

14

Michael collapsed. Phillippe and Nicola caught him.

'Take him over here,' Phillippe said and they dragged him to a chair outside the office and sat him down. Phillippe patted Michael's cheek and leant close to him.

'I will tidy this up as best I can,' he pressed a piece of paper into Michael's hand. 'Call him as soon as you can. Don't go home tonight.'

Phillippe stood up and looked at Nicola and he walked away to direct orders at the other policemen.

'We need to go,' Nicola said and she pulled Michael up. They went down the stairs, Nicola supporting Michael. They went back to the car.

'We need to go somewhere,' Nicola said and she turned to Michael. 'Get it together!'

Nicola turned the car around fast and began to drive along the suburban streets with no idea where she was going.

'Along here,' Michael said. He sounded as if he had taken a blow to the stomach. 'There's a hotel along here.'

Nicola followed his directions. They pulled the car up outside the hotel.

'You have to get it together,' Nicola said. Michael began to compose himself, then he screamed, thumping at the dashboard. Nicola just watched him. There was nothing she could say.

They got out of the car and booked themselves into the hotel. A single room. Nicola didn't want to let him out of her sight. They got to the room. Nicola poured a scotch for Michael.

'Down that and call whoever is on that piece of paper,' Nicola said.

Michael reached into his pocket. He had half-forgotten the piece of paper Phillippe had given him. He downed the scotch and called the number. Michael didn't speak. He listened and then fumbled at a notepad and pen left on a side table and jotted down an address. Under the address he wrote, _bring her_.

Nicola looked at the note and looked into Michael's eyes. He looked lost and she wondered how much longer he would be of use. She had made up her mind though, to walk into the lion's den. She wanted to either succeed or die. She didn't care which and she didn't care about the odds.

'When are we meeting?' she said.

'Tomorrow. Not far from here.'

'We need to eat and rest,' Nicola said. Michael agreed and they ordered the plainest food they could, and they ate it in the room. They hardly spoke. The tension began to dissipate, replaced by a calm resignation of their fates. They finished their meal. Nicola went into the shower, locking the door behind her. She dressed in the bathroom; Michael looked expectant as she came back into the bedroom.

'You need to wash,' she said. Nicola found spare bedding and threw it on the floor. She lay down on the floor fully dressed and pulled the covers over her.

'Sleep well Michael,' she said and she closed her eyes.

15

The next morning, they woke hung over from adrenaline. Neither had the stomach to eat. Nicola saw dread fear in Michael's eyes and wondered if he would break. Without Michael, Nicola wouldn't be able to get any further. She needed to keep him going somehow.

'Get a grip!' she said.

Michael was pallid. He looked deflated and lost.

'Wash and get ready!' she said.

Michael seemed to gather himself. He washed and dressed. It was early. They left the hotel to walk along the cold, dawn streets to the meeting place nearby.

Michael knocked on the door of a building similar to the headquarters. An old door, probably two hundred years old. It was answered by the same tall man who had spoken to Michael's mother the day before. He ushered them in, he didn't speak. He barely looked at Nicola, but she noticed a subtle hint of malice as he looked at Michael.

They followed the man into a side room. It looked like an old dining room. There were two other older men sat at the table. It looked like more would be arriving. There was tension in the air, anger even. Michael's mother must have had information that they didn't have and it seemed clear that they didn't have the chip. The light was faint. The room north facing. The man who had let them into the building switched on the light, but it was of little use. There were no introductions or courtesies. They all sat in a menacing silence, until the silence was broken by a sharp knock on the door and two other older men entered the room. They too were solemn, impolite. They glared without pretence at Michael. They sat. No one looked at each other. They waited. There were half a dozen more knocks at the door and then the tall man stood at the end of the table.

'Let's start,' he said and all eyes turned to Michael. No one spoke, they gazed and waited. It was as if Nicola was invisible. Michael raised his hands off the table, not knowing where to start. An *I don't know* gesture. He cleared his throat.

'My Mother and sister are dead,' he said.

'We know,' one of the men said.

'You were arranging a coup,' another said.

'We need access to everything you have,' said another.

Michael composed himself. He realised he had something on them. He had more knowledge than them, or rather, they thought he did.

'Who's this?' another man spoke and pointed a thumb at Nicola. Without looking at her.

'I'm Nicola,' she said and looked defiantly back at him, though he still didn't meet her stare.

'She's crucial to this,' Michael said. He seemed a little more confidant.

'This is the first time we have all met together,' the tall man at the head of the table said.

'So, we have to get this over with quickly,' one of the others said. They all turned again and looked at Michael.

'You tell me what you know!' Michael said, raising his voice. He was angry and didn't seem to care anymore. He had lost a lot in the last twenty-four hours and the pain was beginning to show. Nicola wondered if he was getting reckless. She looked around the room and tried to memorise the faces of the men around her. They were half shadowed in the dim light. She thought about the possibilities that could unfold if she could kill all of them right here, right now. She knew that they were endangering a great deal by being together. A few of the men looked at her and she felt as if they could see into her thoughts. She didn't look away but softened her gaze. She felt as if it was a game of poker and wanted to advise Michael, but she couldn't risk giving anything away.

'You want Klober's empire, wherever it is,' Michael said. 'I can find it, you know that. I will continue my mother's work.'

The men looked at each other, back and forth, and the tall man at the head of the table spoke.

'You have twenty-four hours,' he said. It seemed like a choreographed response. They had already agreed on what they would say and do. Nicola glanced around again at the shaded faces. They knew more than they let on, but they didn't know where the chip was. The men all got up and left in separate cars, leaving Nicola and Michael alone. Nicola went to speak, but Michael held his finger to his lip in a *shush* gesture.

They got up and left the building. As they turned into another street, Nicola spoke.

'What is this weird family business you have?' she said.

'Had – no family is left now.'

'I'm sorry for what you've lost,' Nicola said. Michael seemed cold and detached. Maybe it just needs to sink in, she thought.

'Why do they need you?' Nicola said.

'We acted like a chairman . . . someone they could communicate through and enact things on their behalf.'

'And take the blame for things that went wrong,' Nicola said. Michael said nothing.

Nicola could see their organisation was flawed, like all of them are. She still didn't understand what had happened between his mother and sister. She didn't really care. She wanted the information off that chip and flashes of rage towards Michael surged through her. She hid her emotions as best she could. Michael stopped and Nicola stopped with him. He looked at her and held her wrist.

'I will find it,' he said. Nicola looked back at him. There was nothing she could say, but she was sure her angry eyes spoke for her.

16

Phillippe answered the call reluctantly. He had a knot in his stomach. He was walking a tightrope and he knew he would lose his balance. It was Michael. He wanted to meet. He was on his way to the station. Phillippe agreed to meet him. Best get it over with, he thought. He looked forward to seeing the woman with him again. This was a little consolation.

Michael and Nicola walked up the steps to the small, local police station and reported at the desk. Phillippe met them and they went up a dingy staircase to a small, drab office. Phillippe slid a file towards Michael. Nicola leant across and took it. She opened it. There was a photo of Peter, the technician from the University, walking along a corridor. Behind it was another photo of him making his way over a fence at the edge of the campus grounds. It enraged Michael. He thought they had abducted Peter.

'Where is he?' Michael said.

'We don't know.'

Nicola scrunched the photo in her hand. Her finger-nails cut through the thick paper and dug into her palm.

Both men looked a little shocked at her rage. She didn't speak. Nicola's head whirled. She had been through so much for nothing.

'We have a day to find this,' Michael said. Phillippe didn't answer. He knew the implications. His duty was to Michael's mother, he hadn't had contact with the rest of the organisation. He presented an annoyance to them. His staff and family did by implication. The organisation never made threats. They didn't have to. But the organisation was desperate, and the three people in this room were their only hope of getting what they wanted. This was the only reason they still lived. Nicola trusted neither man. And she could see they didn't trust each other.

Nicola could see calm resign in the men's eyes and they looked at her, expecting the same. But Nicola was defiant. The men believed they were going to die. It was a look she had seen before. These men were preparing to sacrifice themselves. Phillippe had to protect his family, but why did Michael have to sacrifice himself? He had lost everything. He had nothing left to lose. Maybe he could hide somewhere, for a while at least.

'We have to get that chip,' Nicola said. It snapped the two men out of their trance. Phillippe didn't question her. It was obvious he knew about the chip. The two men agreed with her, silently.

'This is the only lead we have,' Phillippe said, pointing to the scrunched photo, still in Nicola's hand. She looked down at the crumpled photo, her fist still clenched. She was a little shocked by the unconscious power of her feelings. The men didn't seem to question her motives. She wondered why.

'It will be impossible to deal with the Swiss authorities,' Phillippe continued. 'We will have to find a way to deal with this ourselves.'

Michael looked at Phillippe and nodded. 'Where do we start?' he said.

'We can go back and look at his place, but that will be pointless,' Michael said.

'Maybe. But it would be stupid not to try,' Phillippe said. 'There will be something there we may not expect.'

Nicola unfolded the photo and looked at it. She crumpled it up again and threw it across the room.

'What are we waiting for?' she said.

*   *   *

The tall man who had sat at the head of the table was now the organisations unofficial chairman. They didn't need to do anything officially. There was an unbreakable discipline amongst them. It held them all, with menace. Violence was seldom needed. Knowledge was not often shared in any great detail amongst them. The greater aim was all that was important. They were about to share in the knowledge of David Klober's empire though. This was the only thing that had threatened them. Michael and Michelle's mother had been key to obtaining the information on their behalf. Two events had blindsided the organisation though. First, the appearance of Nicola. They had no idea where she had come from. They couldn't

69

fathom how she had got so close to Klober. Second. The death of the former chairman and her daughter. A freak event, or were they connected?

Freak events occur, the tall man had told them. But freak events of this nature, have so much gravity, they attract a multitude of possibilities. We have a huge hole in our knowledge, he had told them. They are the only ones who can fish it out for us. Then we can move on, like we always have and always will.

17

Phillippe's car sped from Paris to the Swiss border. Phillippe had enough authority to gloss over the trip, associating it with another case, firmly within the borders of France. They passed without any effort into Switzerland, making a round trip to the small town and to the apartment owned by Peter. They had the following wind of the organisation.

The apartment building was standard, neat and Swiss. Built in the nineteen fifties. Nothing out of the ordinary. It had a neat, clean entrance. There were a dozen apartments and Peter lived at number eight. They walked unimpeded to his apartment and Phillippe knocked on the door. Phillippe looked around to see if any nosey neighbours would appear, but no one did. He knocked again and listened at the door. There was nothing, no sound of any movement. A thought occurred to Nicola.

'He's a technician right?' she said.

'Yes,' Michael said. 'Why?'

'Could he have booby trapped the place?'

Michael and Phillippe looked at each other. They felt a little stupid and all of them backed away from the door.

'So, what do we do?' Phillippe asked and the three of them stood silently, thinking.

'We can't stand here all day,' Phillippe said and he started to pick the lock. Nicola and Michael stood well out of the way. Phillippe felt the levers move on the lock and tried the handle. The door opened. He pushed the door open a little further. There was no explosion, or any surprises. None yet anyway.

They all sighed, taking a collective intake of breath. Nicola barged past Phillippe and walked into the apartment. It was bright, sparse. It looked as if it was lived in by a single man. There were no photos. The beds were tidy. There were ornaments, neatly arranged.

'This doesn't look right,' Nicola said.

'No, it looks like a show home. Staged,' Phillippe said.

Michael wondered about the apartment and it didn't seem right to him. It didn't seem to reflect what he knew about Peter.

'This place has been ransacked and sanitised,' Phillippe said.

'There's nothing here, we've wasted our time,' Michael said.

Nicola heard the click of a door opening outside in the corridor. She raised her finger to her lips and the two men looked back at her and stood frozen. An old man came to the door. He looked friendly. He was smiling.

'Are you coming to rent the apartment?' he said, casting his eyes over the three of them.

'I'm thinking about it,' Nicola said.

The man looked at them a little while. He seemed to think and then hesitate.

'May I ask your name?' he said, looking at Nicola.

Nicola looked at him, he seemed no threat and she felt compelled to tell him the truth.

'I'm Nicola.'

Michael and Phillippe looked a little annoyed.

'You're not really here to rent the apartment, are you?' he said.

'No,' Nicola said.

She could feel Michael and Phillipe roll their eyes and raise their hands in frustration.

'Peter left something for you,' the old man said. He walked away back to his apartment and he waved them to follow.

'Could be a trap,' Michael said.

'It's too good to be true,' Phillippe said.

Nicola rolled her eyes and followed the old man.

His apartment was the same size as Peter's, except it was a mirror image and full of clutter.

'Take a seat,' he said.

They moved papers and cushions to find room to sit.

'Would you like coffee?' he said. They said yes. They didn't speak whilst the old man was in the kitchen. They were all exhausted. Nicola felt a mix of tension and fatigue. The old man returned from the kitchen with the coffee. Phillippe introduced them.

73

'I'm Ben,' the old man said.

'You said you had something from Peter,' Nicola said.

'Oh yes,' Ben said and he drained his coffee cup and looked around, his face furrowed into a frown. They all cast their eyes around the apartment. It was a mess, more than they had first realised. Ben stood up and stroked his chin. He cast his eyes about. Nicola, Phillippe and Michael felt distraught.

'I told you it was too good to be true,' Phillippe said. He let out a deep sigh.

Phillippe wandered about the living room. He went to the window. It had a good view of the street. He could see their car parked below.

'How well did you know Peter?' Phillippe said.

Ben broke from his concentrated sifting through piles of papers and took a few seconds to comprehend the question.

'I knew him fairly well. He lived here about five years.'

The others were looking around, trying to find something.

'What exactly are we looking for?' Michael said.

'An envelope,' Ben said.

Michael and Nicola looked at each other. They dared to hope that it could be true, that the chip was here.

'What happened to Peter?' Phillippe said.

'He moved, suddenly, yesterday. He didn't even say goodbye.'

'What makes you think he moved?' Nicola said. She held in her hands two old newspapers.

'A truck turned up yesterday and cleared out everything, even the flooring and the kitchen cabinets. There must have been fifty people. There was a lot of banging and sawing. Then another truck turned up and put a load of stuff back.'

'Did any other neighbours see anything?' Phillippe said.

Ben rested his chin on his fist and thought.

'There are no other neighbours,' Ben said.

'Why?' Nicola said.

'I don't know!' Ben said.

'Was there anything else you saw?' Phillippe said.

'No—ah-wait. When I was looking through the spyhole in the door, I looked down and noticed an envelope had been slid under the door.'

Michael let out an exhausted sigh. Ben rummaged around his pockets and took out a crumpled envelope. Nicola tossed the newspapers she was holding back on the pile.

'May I?' she said, holding out her hand to Ben. Ben handed her the crumpled envelope.

Ben sat back down on his chair and the other three sat on the sofa, squeezed tight together. Nicola looked at the envelope. It said: *Give it to the blonde woman who comes looking for me.* Nicola opened it. There was a single piece of paper inside. It said: *Sorry, they got to me, forgive me.*

Michael and Phillippe shut their eyes tight with disappointment. Nicola scrunched the paper tight in her hand. She calmed herself.

'Did you see anything else?' she said.

'I saw Peter getting into a car before the truck arrived.'

Ben got up and walked to the window. He pointed down to their car.

'They were exactly where your car is now,' he said.

'Thank you for your time Ben and for the coffee,' Nicola said and they got up to leave. Nicola held firm onto the crumpled note and envelope. She couldn't bear to let them go. They said their goodbyes and walked out into the hall. Ben shut the door. The latch echoed. They looked at each other. Nicola glared at Michael and Phillippe began to fear for his children. They made their way down the hard steps. They didn't speak. As they got to the entrance, they heard the latch click and echo. They stopped and listened, then Nicola slowly made her way back up the stairs. Ben was about to close the door again.

'Ben?' Nicola said. She hurried her step. Ben opened the door again.

'Oh good, you are still here,' he said.

Nicola climbed the last few steps back onto the landing.

'Was there something else?' she said.

'Something else? Oh, yes, something else.'

'We need to go,' Michael's harsh voice echoed up to them. She could hear that Phillippe had started the car.

'Was there something else?' Nicola said again.

'I wrote down the number plate of the car.'

Nicola's eyes widened and she felt her heart palpitate. Ben pointed to the crumpled-up paper in Nicola's hand and closed the door.

18

Phillippe wanted to get out of there. As soon as they were in the car he drove, not knowing where he was going.

'I will see what I can do,' Phillippe said. 'But I will need your help Michael, it is out of my jurisdiction.'

Michael held the envelope and began to send a message with his phone. Nicola sat in the back and looked over his shoulder.

'Stop,' she said.

'Why?' Michael said, he stopped typing.

'I know that registration plate.'

Phillippe pulled the car over. They were in a quiet street at the edge of town. The lake and mountains in the distance. Light snow fell.

'The man who took the chip from me, when I woke in hospital, he drove away in that car.'

Michael and Phillippe looked again at the registration number.

'It's one of your cars Michael,' Nicola said.

'My mother sent it. She would have kept it all to herself.'

'There was nothing in your mother's office,' Phillippe said.

Michael felt a pang of fear about the secret he shared with Michelle. He wondered if Phillippe knew. He felt ashamed that his fear of their secret was greater than his grief for Michelle.

'We found nothing,' Phillippe said again, as if he had read Michael's mind.

'Does anyone know what is going on in your . . . organisation?' Nicola said.

'We have a common goal, but individual actions are kept to the individual,' Michael said.

'I expect you all thought that was a flawless strategy?' Phillippe said.

Michael said nothing for a while and then said: 'You found the man who took the chip from you. How?'

Nicola thought back. Her head had been fuzzy when she woke from the hospital bed. The registration plate of the black Mercedes was clear. It was the same car that had taken Peter. She had watched it drive away and remembered her screams. The nurse calming her.

'You wouldn't believe me if I told you,' she said.

Nicola thought back to how she had gathered her belongings and got dressed. The doctor and two nurses had tried to calm her. They tried to get her to stay. She had asked them how she had got there. They told her that she had been dropped off by private ambulance and that was all they knew. She asked them if they had been given any medical records, there must be some paper trail? She said: 'You must have something about me?' But they had nothing or wouldn't reveal anything. They knew nothing of the man who had just visited her.

Nicola made her final barge past them and left. She walked out of the hospital and out of the carpark. She was in Switzerland. The staff had spoken French. Last time she was conscious, she was on a beach in the Caribbean. Probably the Bahamas. She had lit a signal fire.

Her head was spinning, she couldn't really remember much of the conversation she had just had with the medics, but she knew she was underdressed, and she was cold. She walked up a street that hugged the hospital grounds, to a junction with traffic lights. A van pulled up and two men grabbed her and threw her in the back. She was almost collapsing. She later learned that she had been in an induced coma and had somehow brought herself out of it. No wonder she was feeling woozy. She relayed all of this to Michael and Phillippe.

'I thought they were taking me back to the hospital,' she said.

Michael looked ashamed. He is too soft for his job, Nicola thought.

Michael's phone buzzed and he looked at a message.

'They are meeting again tomorrow, all of them, they want me there regardless,' Michael said.

Phillippe gripped the wheel tighter. What had he got himself into? he thought.

'I wish your mother wasn't such a persuasive woman,' Phillippe said.

81

Michael said nothing but wondered what his mother had done to force Phillippe into submission. Money would have been involved, but they always used more than money. His mother seemed to know how to use love, pervert its use anyway. She had once told them it was the most powerful currency. It was strange he thought. Because she knew nothing about love.

'The car was sent from your organisation. Can't you trace it?' Nicola said.

'This was solely my mother's doing. And she's dead,' Michael said.

'I'm sorry,' Nicola said, though she hesitated.

'Don't be,' Michael said.

'I don't know how we can find it. Situation was different last time,' Nicola said.

'Tell us how you did it last time,' Phillippe said.

Nicola told them how she was in the van and they hadn't tied her wrists or restrained her in any way. They didn't think they would need to. The van had benches running parallel with the sides. The two men were young, maybe mid-twenties. They were silent, proud, a little fanatical she thought. There was a driver. There was no bulkhead between the driver and the back. They were all dressed in everyday clothes, but they had that military look. The driver was older, probably in charge. She guessed they were all armed, probably Beretta pistols. Nicola leant forward to look ahead, through the windshield. The guard next to her pushed her back without turning his head to look at her. This made Nicola very angry, but she buried it for the meantime. Nicola sat to the left of the man next to her. His opposite number sat directly opposite her. She looked at his torso, looking for the bulge of the pistol, was he left or right-handed?

Nicola didn't speak, she knew there was no point trying to break the silent act they were all putting on. She shuffled up tighter to the man next to her. She tried to see if his pistol was strapped to the side closest to her. It was, but it was too awkward to get to. Both men wore puffy jackets, zipped up. Their pistols would be awkward for them to get as well. Nicola still felt weak and woozy. She thought about whether it would be best to let them take her to wherever she was going. They might lead her back to the chip. She managed a sideways glance through the windshield and could see that they were heading deeper into the countryside. They were going somewhere remote to dispose of her. They got to some winding mountain roads, not quite Alpine, must be the Jura, Nicola thought. The roads wound their way through passes that could give you more of a chance if you crashed down them. Her thoughts were broken by the buzz of the driver's phone. He held it to his ear, listened, said OK and closed the call.

'They need her to work out what's on the chip,' he said. This increased the tension in the two men in the back. Their job just got a little more complicated. They were psyching themselves up for murder. Now they had to protect and deliver.

The van didn't seem to change direction. They seemed to be continuing on the same course. The driver's phone buzzed again. This time a text. 'Ten minutes, he will meet us there tonight,' he relayed to his comrades. Nicola now needed the vehicle intact. She had to change her plan and go with the flow.

19

'What's so unbelievable about that, I've seen what you're capable of?' Michael said.

'I haven't finished,' Nicola said.

'Shall we just sit here all day or are you going to tell us how to find this car?' Phillippe said.

'You will have to use me as bait,' Nicola said.

'How?' Phillippe said.

'Michael, or rather his mother, or his organisation used me before with Klober. The first time I met your lot, that's what they did.'

Michael shrugged; he didn't know anything about it.

'They have Peter, and he will show them how to read the chip,' Michael said.

'But they don't have him do they, or they wouldn't need us, we wouldn't still be alive,' Phillippe said.

'They must be somewhere, waiting to hear from my mother.'

'Or they could have a breakaway faction,' Nicola said.

'What happened between my sister and mother?' Michael said. He felt his heart start to race and his skin prickle as he asked.

'You want to know the details?' Phillippe said.

Michael nodded, though he dreaded what he was about to hear.

'There was an argument in your mother's office. Michelle left, shaking. She went to the toilet, she came back, holding the porcelain lid from the cistern, went into your mother's office and beat her own mother to death with it. She then took a cell phone out of your mother's desk drawer and smashed it to tiny pieces. She picked up a shard of porcelain and cut her own throat.'

Michael got out of the car and vomited. Nicola followed him to try and comfort him.

'Why did she do that, Michael?' she said.

Michael waved her away and continued to retch. Nicola got back into the car.

'We have no idea what goes on with them,' Phillippe said.

'You could have sanitised the story a little,' Nicola said.

'I did,' Phillippe said.

Phillippe lowered the window and gave Michael a cloth.

'It's clean, there are bottles of water in the back,' he said.

Michael wiped his mouth and tossed the rag. He rinsed his mouth with the water and tossed the bottle. He took a few deep breaths and got into the car.

Phillippe gave him a mint.

'What was that machine in the room Peter locked us in?' Michael said.

'An AFM, but that was just a ruse,' Nicola said.

'I don't think so, I saw the look in his eye, it looked like a eureka moment, I think that's why he ran when he did.'

Phillippe looked AFM up on his phone. He held up a photo of the machine that looked like the one at the university.

'Atomic Force Microscope,' Phillippe said.

'That's it, that must be how we can read the chip,' Nicola said.

'They will need one and that's how we will find them,' Phillippe said.

'We need the organisation's help,' Michael said.

'As soon as you tell them what to look for, we will be redundant and dead,' Phillippe said. He wasn't thinking of himself though.

'Would he go back and use the one at the university?' Nicola said.

'It's a possibility,' Michael said.

'What if he is waiting for some kind of signal though? He must have someone with him, they must be waiting too,' Nicola said.

'We don't have time to wait,' Phillippe said.

They were silent, thinking, scared. Nicola felt she had the most to lose, but she knew she didn't. She felt a little sorry for Phillippe.

'We don't have any time to find every AFM he could use,' Nicola said.

'But what if he doesn't go anywhere? He is probably waiting for your mother to contact him, or more likely, the people he is with are. I think Nicola is right,' Phillippe said.

'You said that Peter looked like he had a eureka moment,' Nicola said.

'Yes,' Michael said.

'That might give us our chance,' Nicola said.

The two men looked at her expectantly.

'He won't be able to resist taking a look,' she said.

'He thinks we are long gone too, so he won't expect us,' Michael said.

'What if his handlers are with him? They'll not let the chip out of their sight,' Phillippe said.

'We will deal with that if we have to,' Nicola said.

'So how do we proceed?' Phillippe said.

'We can't show our faces,' Michael said.

'He doesn't know me,' Phillippe said.

'Phillippe can call him,' Nicola said.

'Peter doesn't have a phone,' Michael said.

'Do you think he is working as normal at the University?' Nicola said.

They stopped talking and thought for a while.

'I'm the only one who can find out, but I will need some help from your organisation Michael,' Phillippe said.

'I'll see what I can do,' Michael said.

20

The tall, sombre man took the call.

'Yes Michael.'

'I need to help someone impersonate a Swiss policeman.'

'Is he trusted?'

'Of course.'

'Send me the details. I will see to it.'

'Thank you.'

'Michael.'

'Yes.'

'You know you must settle matters quickly.'

He hung up. Nicola and Phillippe looked at Michael, who tapped some information into his phone.

'Thank you for doing this Phillippe,' Nicola said. She knew that he was exposing himself to the greater organisation. This was either a curse or blessing to Phillippe.

'Let's go somewhere more comfortable,' Michael said.

They drove to a nearby cafe. Michael decided to avoid the usual places. They sat down at a table near the window and Michael sent another message and they ordered coffee and something to eat.

'You OK eating?' Phillippe said to Michael.

'I feel OK now.'

Their food and coffee arrived. They sank into their chairs, craving sleep.

'A courier is bringing your new credentials,' Michael said to Phillippe.

He turned to Nicola, who was eating as if she hadn't seen food for a week.

'What?' she said.

'Tell us how you got the chip in the first place,' Michael said.

'You got to the point where you were in the van,' Phillippe said.

'You said we wouldn't believe you,' Michael said.

'One thing I've learned about you people, is that power blinds you,' she said.

They looked at her a little confused.

'You expect to win all the time. You don't see, or even prepare for defeat,' she said.

Michael looked pensive. He was silent.

'So, what happened?' Phillippe said.

Nicola fought the urge to attack the driver and bring the van crashing over the hillside. It was too risky. Now she had a chance of finding the chip again, so it would be pointless and stupid. She hated inaction. It felt too much like submission.

The van pulled up a gravel road and then stopped. They manhandled her out of the van. They were outside an isolated cabin. Snow was beginning to fall. The area around it was open. There were clumps of spruce around on the horizon. She still wasn't tied up. Her hands and feet were still free. They led her inside. They sat her at a table.

And this was the unbelievable part.

On the table was a fully loaded, long barrelled M24 sniper rifle, with all the accessories. Nicola thought she was part of some practical joke.

'Seriously?' Michael said.

'Seriously,' Nicola said and she drained her cup of coffee. Her plate was clear, the other two had hardly started their food. They wondered how Nicola could talk and eat so fast.

'And a bowie knife,' she said.

Phillippe choked on his coffee. It was the first time he had smiled in days. Michael looked at his plate. He took a mouthful of food, swallowed and looked at Nicola.

'Why do you want this so bad?' he said.

Nicola tried to speak but couldn't find the words. Phillippe looked at her and decided to change the subject.

'When is the courier arriving?' he said. Michael got the hint.

'Soon,' he said.

Nicola excused herself and went to the toilet. She shut the cubicle door and wept as quietly as she could. She left the cubicle, splashed her face and composed herself and went back to the table. No one spoke, and eventually a motorcycle courier arrived and walked into the cafe.

Phillippe stood up and took the package from him. The owner of the cafe looked at them suspiciously.

'We need to make a move,' Phillippe said. They went back to the car and drove to another side street. Phillippe opened the package. It contained Swiss federal police identification and login details to a server that could create electronic warrants.

'Okay?' Michael said.

'Very okay,' Phillippe said. He tucked the identification card into his wallet, took a photograph of the login details and then put them and his phone into his pocket.

'You need to stay out of the way. I'm going to do this now. What is Peter's surname?'

'Peter Böhm,' Michael said.

'Böhm?' Nicola said. The name shocked her and meant a great deal. She felt stupid for giving away how much it meant to her. Phillippe noticed, but he said nothing.

'Just sounds familiar,' Nicola said. She thought again of her meeting with Peter. He seemed unfriendly, but now she wondered if he recognised her, or at least recognised her similarity to someone else.

'Let's go,' Phillippe said. They drove near to the university.

'You take the car. I will walk from here. The French plates will look suspicious,' Phillippe said.

They dropped him off and wished him good luck.

'My luck is your luck also,' he said. They turned the car around and drove away.

'I can't stand this,' Nicola said. 'I want to be there.'

'We have no choice,' Michael said. Nicola knew it was true.

'He may not even be there. He could be waiting in some sink hole somewhere,' Michael said. Or he could be dead, Nicola thought. They drove to the lake and got out and looked over the grey water. Neither spoke.

21

Phillipe walked with authority to the gate at the front of the university. He showed his identification.

'I'm looking for Peter Böhm,' he said. Phillippe looked at the gate and the guardhouse and wondered about the excessive security. The guard was friendly, in awe, a wannabe policeman. He pointed Phillippe to the right building and let him in. Phillippe walked up to the concierge, showed his ID and asked for Peter.

'About yesterday?' the concierge said.

'Yes'

'Follow me.'

Phillippe's pulse rose a little. The anticipation of a hunter about to make his kill. The concierge led him to the lab.

'Peter, a policeman to see you,' the concierge whispered.

Peter looked up. A flash of horror crossed his face and then he quickly suppressed it.

'I put off the Police,' he said. 'I told them it was a misunderstanding.'

'A misunderstanding about what?' Phillippe said.

The concierge lingered and Peter glared at him, so he walked back to his post. Peter looked flustered. He hadn't been prepared for this visit. Phillippe could see his brain scrabble around for an answer.

'The door shut and locked itself, I couldn't find the key, and one of them had claustrophobia and panicked.'

'So, who and where are these people?'

Beads of sweat began to form on Peter's head.

'Friends.'

Phillippe stared directly into Peter's eyes and shrugged. 'And?'

'Just friend's, they came to look at the AFM.'

'I need their names and contact details.'

Phillippe could almost feel the heat glowing out of Peter. His armpits were now wet, his face was flushed and sweating.

Phillippe leant over Peter.

'Give me the chip,' he said, almost growling.

Peter pushed back away from him and fell off his chair. Phillippe picked up the chair and sat on it, looming over Peter.

'I don't have it . . . I don't have it,' he held up his hand and crawled against the wall. Phillippe unbuttoned his jacket. Peter looked at the handgun in its holster.

'Tell me where it is,' he said.

Phillippe reached into his jacket and Peter shut his eyes and held both hands up, facing his palms out. Phillippe took out his phone and sent a message to Michael.

'Get up, you are coming with me,' Phillippe said. Peter did as he was told. Phillippe turned him around and handcuffed him behind his back.

'Walk,' he said.

Phillippe led a whimpering Peter out of the building. Neither man acknowledged anyone. As he led him out through the gate, Phillippe nodded to the smiling guard, who opened the gate. Nicola and Michael stood by the car and Peter looked horrified. They threw him in the back and drove away fast. Nicola sat in the front and Phillippe was driving. Michael was in the back with Peter.

'Speak to me Peter,' Michael said.

'It was your mother,' Peter said.

'I know. I guess you and her other acolytes are waiting to hear from her?'

Peter nodded.

'Where are they?' Michael said.

Peter shook his head. Michael punched him hard in the ear. He grabbed Peter's jaw and looked deep into his eyes.

'Mother is dead and we have very little time,' Michael said and pushed Peter away. His head hit the side window. Nicola turned and looked at Peter.

'Are they at the cabin?' she said. She saw the flash in Peter's eyes and knew that's where they were. Peter nodded.

'Is the chip there too?' Michael said and Peter affirmed this.

97

'I know the way,' Nicola said. She directed Phillippe.

'We can get there in about an hour,' she said.

'Are we finished with him?' Phillippe said. Michael looked at Peter.

'I'm finished with him,' he said. Peter pissed himself. Michael moved away from him and looked at him with greater disgust.

'No. I need to talk to him,' Nicola said. Phillippe wondered what it was that she knew about him. But he didn't have the space in his mind to care right now.

'If you are lying to us, you will die,' Michael said to Peter.

'You're not leading us into a trap are you Peter?' Phillippe said.

Michael shook his head. Sweat flew from his nose.

'If I discovered you had the chip on you all along, or that it was at the university, you will have a bad death,' Phillippe said.

Nicola turned and looked at Peter. She thought he was telling the truth.

'How are we going to do this?' she said.

'I will have to drop you off and drive there and then I will knock on the door and find out all I can,' Phillippe said.

'That's too risky,' Michael said. He turned and looked at Peter: 'How many of them are there?'

'Two,' Peter said.

'You lie, you die,' Nicola said and she looked at him and smiled.

Peter was starting to shake, almost poisoned by the level of adrenaline in his blood. Good, Nicola thought, I need him softened up. They twisted and turned up the winding, greasy roads that Nicola half recognised. The snow was thicker as they increased altitude.

'Pull over here,' she said.

Phillippe pulled the car into a small layby. Woodland stretched up a steep bank. She told Phillippe where to find the cabin.

'What will you do?' she said.

'I will improvise,' Phillippe said. Nicola flashed him a look of concern and he smiled.

Nicola and Michael dragged Peter out of the car and walked him up the bank. The snow hadn't made it through the canopy, but it was very cold. They sat in the undergrowth. They flanked Peter, who shivered from fear and cold. His backside wet.

They watched Phillippe drive away. Nicola felt helpless again. Michael looked pale and agitated.

'Who was that old lady who tried to poison me?' she said.

Michael took a little while to break from his thoughts.

'Some operative of my mother's,' he said.

'How did you know I would go there?' she said.

'We didn't, I guessed that was the one you would go to . . .'

A car neared on the road below. Peter kicked forward and rolled down the bank, crashing through the undergrowth. Nicola saw a Volvo, its lights on. It was driving fast.

Nicola and Michael ducked out of sight. The car slowed as it approached the shuddering line of undergrowth.

* * *

Phillippe pulled up to the cabin. The Black Mercedes with the Zurich plates was parked outside. He knew that he had been spotted. He knocked on the door and stood to the side of it. It was eventually answered by a man in his thirties. He was wearing a check shirt. Phillippe could see that he had some kind of discreet body armour underneath.

'Police,' Phillippe said, he held up the ID. The man stepped aside and let him in.

22

Nicola scrambled down the bank after Peter. He had tangled into a large shrub twenty feet from the road. Nicola clamped her hand over his mouth. She lay on top of him and kneed him in the balls.

'I will kill you like David killed your father,' she said. Peter looked at her, amazed? Puzzled? She couldn't tell, but there was certainly recognition of some truth. The Volvo stopped. Michael kept low. His heart pounding into the ground, Nicola clamped her hand tighter around Peter's mouth and pushed her knee harder into his balls. She felt the stifled yelp under her hand. The Volvo's engine idled. The window opened three inches. A camera lens protruded from it. Peter and Nicola held their breath. She could feel Peter's breath rasp between her fingers. She flashed him another look that said *Shut up*.

The camera lens trained towards the place where Peter and Nicola hid. The car lingered for an age and Nicola and Michael still held their breath. The door opened a crack. A foot appeared. Nicola heard a voice, she picked out the words *bear* and *wolf*. The door closed and the

Volvo drove away. They breathed again. Nicola sat up and pushed her knee into Peter's chest.

'You do that again and I will kill you,' she said.

Her eyes were wild with rage. She burned with hatred for the thief. Peter blinked and she took this as acknowledgement. She got him up and almost dragged him back up the slope. Michael clambered down and helped her. They threw Peter down.

'Take off his shoes,' Nicola said. They took off his shoes and tossed them, then Michael took of his socks, balled them up and pushed them into Peter's mouth.

'Now shut the fuck up,' Nicola said.

Nicola checked his cuffs. His wrists were sore, he had been trying to free himself from them. Peter's eyes widened. He was struggling for breath. Nicola pulled the socks out of his mouth and stuffed them in his jacket pocket. He sucked air into his lungs.

'You are David Klober's step-brother,' Nicola said. Michael looked shocked. Peter nodded. Nicola looked at Michael.

'You didn't know this?' she said.

'Everything went through my mother,' Michael said.

'His mother know about you?' Nicola said.

'Yes,' Peter said.

Michael looked down at the ground and shook his head. He felt angry and stupid. He was out of his league. He would never be able to take over the organisation. His mother had been right.

'You must have enough money—what did she have over you?' Michael said.

'My life.'

'Did you help him make the chip?' Nicola said.

'Yes,' Peter said.

'Do you know what's on it?' Michael said.

'Yes.'

'Is it the only one?' Nicola said.

'Yes.'

Nicola looked directly at Peter.

'What is on it?' she said.

23

Phillippe sat on a soft chair towards the middle of the room. Hard to get out of quickly and easy for someone to sneak behind. This is why he had been offered this chair and he knew it. The man who had let him in sat on a high stool and leant his elbow on a high countertop. Quick to spring from, good cover of the room.

'You out here on your own?' Phillippe said.

'Yes, I'm a photographer.'

'What are you photographing?'

'The spruces, it's for an article on violins.'

Phillippe frowned.

'The timber round here is used to make the best of them,' the man said.

'I thought that was further north,' Phillippe said.

The man shifted on the stool.

'Hard to get accommodation this time of year, this is the closest I could get.'

'I see, Mr . . .?'

'Banks—can I ask what it is you want?'

'Missing person, woman, blonde, young. She was last seen around here.'

Mr Banks scratched the back of his head.

'Can't help you there,' he said.

'What's that?' Phillippe said.

'What?'

'I heard someone else.' Phillippe had heard no one, but he knew someone else was there. Mr Banks was making a good job of hiding his tension. Phillippe stared at him and narrowed his eyes, he said nothing.

'Look . . . I can't help you,' Mr Banks said.

Phillippe said nothing and continued to stare at the man. He let his stare linger a while longer and then cast his eyes around the room.

'That looks like a bullet hole in that wall,' Phillippe said, pointing at the hole. Mr Banks turned to look. Phillippe watched him. As Mr Banks turned his gaze back to Phillippe, he looked at the doorway behind Phillippe. Phillippe stood up out of the chair. Mr Banks was getting a little flustered now. He glanced again at the door behind Phillippe.

'Tell your colleague to stand down, Mr Banks.'

A male voice came from behind Phillippe: 'Why does a Swiss cop have French plates on his car?'

24

'Should we get Phillippe out of there? Do we still need the chip?' Michael said.

'No, we still need it,' she said.

'What's on it?' Michael said.

'Coordinates, locations, bank accounts, plans for his other tech,' Peter said.

'Did my mother know we were going to bring it to you?'

'Yes.'

'Why did they tear your apartment to pieces and rebuild it?' Nicola said.

'I had a lot of stuff there, stuff to do with David.'

'Did you have something in there that can read the chip?' Michael said.

'Yes.'

Michael felt stupid again. Outmanoeuvred by his mother and Peter.

'Where is that machine?' Nicola said.

'I don't know.'

'Where do you think it might be?' Nicola said.

'I don't know.'

'Those two at the cabin. Will they know?' Michael said.

'I think so,' Peter said.

Michael wanted to ask Nicola about what she knew about Peter, but he didn't want to speak in front of him. His little knowledge of the situation was humiliating enough.

'We have to wait and see what Phillippe turns up,' Michael said.

'Have you memorised what's on the chip?' Nicola said.

'It's too much, and I'm sure there is more information hidden on there,' Peter said.

'I thought you helped him make it, you should know,' Michael said.

'I followed his instructions, some of the things he told me to put on it made no sense.'

Michael felt pensive. He wondered if there was any point in what he was doing. He knew that the organisation wouldn't spare his life. They wouldn't spare any of them. He thought of Michelle. The grief and guilt were too overwhelming.

'I want to move closer to the cabin,' Nicola said.

'What about when Phillippe comes back?' Michael said.

'If we cross over the road and go up the opposite bank, we should see the cabin and the road.'

That's a stretch, especially with him,' Michael said.

'You stay here with him,' Nicola said.

'You can uncuff me, I won't run,' Peter said. They ignored him.

'I don't want to stay with him, waiting,' Michael said.

'I can't sit *here* waiting,' Nicola said. She got up and made her way to the road.

'Get up,' Michael said. He stood up and pulled Peter to his feet. They almost tumbled down the bank. They made their way to the road. By the time they had crossed it, Nicola was way up the opposite bank. They followed the trail she made. The hill was steep and hard going. Nicola made it to the top. She could see the cabin, the Mercedes and Phillippe's car outside.

Michael caught up with her. He was almost dragging Peter. Both men were exhausted. Michael was disappointed by the distant view of the cabin. Nicola strained her eyes and wished she had binoculars. The snow here had made it through the trees, and they were all getting colder and wetter. Peter's bare feet were pink and bloodied. Michael had dumped him uncomfortably on the ground, face down, his cramped arms still cuffed behind his back.

'He don't look so good,' Michael said. Nicola didn't really hear him. She stared at the distant cabin. Michael tapped her on the shoulder. Nicola jumped. Michael pointed at Peter, who was silent.

'He don't look so good,' he said again. Nicola looked at him. Peter looked wretched, pathetic and pale under his scratched and bloodied face.

'We are going to need to get him warm,' she said. Nicola needed to ask him a great deal. She turned to look at the cabin again.

'Phillippe needs to hurry up,' she said.

* * *

Phillippe turned and looked behind him. A man in his forties pointed a pistol at him. He looked at Phillippe and motioned for him to hand over his gun. Phillippe slowly reached into his jacket and pulled out his pistol with two fingers and tossed in onto the soft chair. The other man frisked him whilst the man in his forties picked up Phillippe's pistol, checked it and then tucked it in his belt.

'Sit back down,' he said.

Phillippe did as he was told, but in his own time and not before he had buttoned up his jacket. Both men stood over him, either side.

'Who are you?' the older man said.

Phillippe wasn't afraid. Not for himself. But he thought of his family and colleagues. He thought of the limited time he had to get the organisation the information they needed.

'You have a man, Peter, he has something. I need it,' Phillippe said.

The older man waved his pistol at Phillippe.

'Keep talking,' he said.

'You are waiting for someone to contact you. I am your contact.'

The older man flicked the safety on his pistol and put it back in his holster.

Phillippe took a chance.

25

'I'm tired of waiting,' Nicola said and she stood up. 'You wait here, with him.'

'What? . . . you can't go down there!' Michael said.

'I can.'

Nicola walked away from Michael and took a circular route to the cabin. She kept inside the tree line. She had to get through thick scrub quite heavy with snow. As she neared the cabin she tried to get into a position where she could see through a window. The cabin was in a good place, clear of trees all around and difficult to approach without being seen.

Something bugged her. It was too quiet, too inactive. It began to prey on her mind so much that she had to take a risk. She found a good position at the south east corner of the cabin. Out of direct view from the windows. She dashed across the snow and hugged tight up to the wall of the cabin. Her heart pounded. She pressed the back of her head hard against the wall.

Michael saw her distant shape approach the cabin. His heart pounded. If she died, he would be out of the game. He would be stuck with what to do with Peter. He would have to run, but they would get him in a matter of days. He became aware of the power his mother had held. Only now was he aware of that protection. He wanted to run. He looked at Peter, who was turning from pale to blue and he stood up to go. Peter opened his eyes to look up at him and a gunshot echoed from the cabin.

The gunshot came from inside the cabin the same instant a window smashed just round the corner from Nicola. She heard the grunting sounds and thumps of struggle and decided now was the only chance she had. She ran round to the back door of the cabin and tried it, but it was locked, then she saw a window that looked like she might be able to prize open. She looked about for something to open it with, but the area was covered with snow. There was a pile of firewood stacked against the wall the other side of the window. Nicola grabbed a log from the top of the pile and used it as a hammer to smash in the glass. She climbed through, almost leapt. Two men were beginning to overpower Phillippe. He held the arm of one of the men, who held a pistol and wrestled with him. Another man rained blows on Phillippe. None of them noticed her.

Nicola sprinted at the man throwing the punches. She dived at him and wrapped her arms tight around his legs. He crashed to the ground. Nicola sunk her teeth into his thigh. He screamed. Phillippe now had a chance with the other man, but he was losing. Nicola was struggling to grip onto the man's legs, and he was thumping wildly on the back of Nicola's head. She couldn't see if Phillippe was okay. She bit harder and tasted blood. She was growing tired.

Michael stood over Peter, looked at the cabin and then looked down the bank. He could walk to town or hitch-hike he thought. He looked at his phone and switched it off. It was encrypted, it couldn't be tracked, but he couldn't be sure. He left Peter there and started to make his way back down the bank, almost tripping with every step. He got halfway down when his conscience hit him.

Phillippe was losing. His assailant was now starting to point the gun at Phillippe's face. Phillippe shook his head from side to side, growled like an animal about to die and gripped the gunman's hand with slippery, bloodied fingers. *Bang.* Phillippe only heard the first nanosecond of the shot. His ears then rang and that was all he could hear. Nicola jumped at the shot. She bit even harder and clawed her hands into the man's thighs. He still thumped at her and it hurt. She gripped tighter, he screamed. Nicola clawed her way up the man's body and headbutted him in the groin, three times in a quick burst. It took a few seconds for the pain to sink in.

When it did, she climbed onto his chest and punched him in the throat. His larynx cracked and he clutched his throat and gargled. She turned to see Phillippe being overcome. His assailant pointed the gun towards Phillippe's bloodied face. Nicola leapt at him and grabbed his arm. Phillippe took a few long moments to orientate and then grabbed the man around the neck. Both of them pulled him to the ground. The other man still gargled and struggled for breath. He was moving about too much for Nicola's liking, she aimed the other man's hand, still clutching the gun at him, squeezed and shot him in the side of the head. Rage filled her and she smashed her head into the bridge of his nose, it crunched against her forehead. He spluttered and fell unconscious. Phillippe collapsed on his back, still deaf from the ringing in his ears. Nicola tried to get up but fell onto her backside and then lay on her back panting.

Michael appeared at the broken window.

'You OK?' he said.

26

Nicola lay there for a minute and then gathered her strength. She sat upright, her vision a little blurry. She saw Michael climbing through the broken window.

'Where's Peter?' she said.

'Back at the top of the hill, I had to leave him to get down here.'

Phillippe made attempts to climb up from the floor. His hearing was starting to come back. He looked at the body of the man near him and the breathing, unconscious man who was nearer. He checked his pockets for spare handcuffs, but there were none.

'We need to tie him up,' Phillippe said.

Nicola glanced at Michael, who began to look around for some rope.

'Try their bags,' she said, panting with exhaustion and gesturing towards three large duffel bags. Nicola cast her eyes around the cabin. It was such a short time ago she was last here, but it seemed an age. She never expected to see it again. She shuddered, thinking she was trapped in some loop, impossible to escape from.

Michael opened one of the duffel bags. It was packed tight with spare clothes. He tipped it out and rummaged through the clothes. Something bulky was left in the bag, but it was just a spare set of boots. He tipped the two other bags open. One had much the same as the first, but the other had something else.

'You need to hurry,' Nicola said. The unconscious man was coming around. Nicola whipped him across the temple with his pistol. He groaned, she hit him again. He didn't groan and she rolled him on his side, took off his boots, took out the laces and used them to tie his hands and ankles.

'Don't worry, I've done it,' she said. It wasn't perfect, but it would do for now.

'I'm going to see if Peter is still around,' she glowered at Michael, who didn't pay attention to her. He was rummaging through the contents of the last duffel bag. It irritated her further. She slammed the door behind her when she left.

It was beginning to snow again. She walked a direct route towards Peter. She looked beyond the cabin and could see the narrow valley beyond where she retrieved the chip not so long ago. The clump of spruce trees was shrouded in a misty snow cloud that crept towards the cabin, so she hurried up. She made it to the spot where Peter should be. There was a trace of blood in the snow and a trail that she followed a short way. She found Peter. He had shuffled his way about twenty yards. He was dead.

Peter was still cuffed behind his back. If someone found him like that, it would cause more trouble. She had forgotten to bring the key. She looked down at the cabin and at the snow cloud descending down the valley. She grabbed his feet under her arm and dragged him back to cabin. By the time she got there, the cabin was shrouded in mist and the snow was falling quite hard. She banged on the door.

Michael opened it to a breathless, furious Nicola. She barged past him, dragging the cold corpse and dropping its feet on the floor.

'Not much use to us now,' she said. Phillippe was still recovering and shook his head, fearful of how much this would delay them. Michael sighed and looked down. In his hand was a small box that looked like a small military computer. It had a robust, shock proof case around it. It was about the size of an SLR camera.

'What's that?' Nicola said.

'I think this is what we need,' Michael said. Nicola walked over to him and took the box from him. She felt a weight lift, her instincts telling her it was true, and she fell into the soft chair without taking her eyes from the box.

Phillippe was quiet, but now up and about. He took the cuffs from Peter's body and pointlessly checked for a pulse. He searched through his pockets, finding only his wallet and car keys. He put both in his pocket. Snow blustered through the broken window. It was getting cold inside. The snow fell heavily. Michael and Phillippe looked out and then looked at each other.

'We won't make it back in time,' Phillippe said.

'I can call them,' Michael said. His phone had no signal. Phillippe checked his. Same problem. They searched the body of the soldier and his now groaning comrade, but they didn't have phones. They searched around but there was nothing.

'We are going to have to stay here,' Nicola said, still transfixed by the box.

'But we could be here for days,' Phillippe said. His anxiety betraying him.

Nicola got up and looked at the deepening snow. It was forming a small drift on the floor beneath the window.

'If we can get to the bigger roads, we should be okay,' she said. 'Take everything useful.'

'What about him?' Michael said, pointing to the groaning soldier.

Nicola walked up to him.

'Do you know about this?' she said, waving the box in front of him.

'Fuck you,' he said through swollen bloodied lips. The remains of his nose streaming blood.

She turned to Phillippe.

'Does he look like the type that will break?' she said.

'I don't think so,' Phillippe said. He pulled his pistol, racked it and pointed it at the soldier's face. The soldier showed no emotion. I'm probably a dead man anyway, the soldier thought, if they find out I failed. This wasn't true though. Michael's mother was the only link to him. He could be free.

'Last chance,' Phillippe said, concentrating his aim on his forehead. The soldier smiled as best he could and spat on the floor. Phillippe shot him through the head. Michael jumped. Nicola watched him twitch until the twitching stopped.

'Let's go,' she said.

'Shall we burn the place?' Michael said.

Nicola looked at Phillippe, who shrugged and thought a few seconds.

'May attract attention too soon,' he said.

Nicola agreed with him, though she would have loved to see the place burn.

Michael fumbled in his pocket. He had found something else in the duffel bags.

27

Phillippe's car only just made it up the track. They had to get out and push a couple of times, but they made it to the road, and it was clear, spotless. Switzerland.

'We will be late,' Michael said. Phillippe agreed but was worried.

'Do we have what we need?' Phillippe said.

'Yes,' Nicola said. She opened the box and held up a small flap which revealed the chip. She recognised it as if it was a part of her.

'Will that be good enough for them?' Phillippe said.

'They can figure out how to use it,' Michael said. He deliberately avoided answering Phillippe directly. He knew that it was no use to the three of them. Their fate was sealed. But, he thought, for the slimmest of chances. Michael checked his phone. The signal still wasn't strong enough.

'I need to tell them we will be slightly delayed,' he said.

The three of them were quiet. Tension silenced them. Nicola could feel it from the other two. It made her feel more on edge. They all eased a little when they crossed the border. Michael was able to send a message. It was received at the other end, but there was no reply. They were exhausted and took turns driving. They arrived at the outskirts of Paris at dusk. A message came through to Michael to meet at the old headquarters. His stomach knotted. He thought he would never see the old building again.

Phillippe was driving. He parked the car a little way from the building. Nicola clutched the box.

'I'm going with you,' she said. Michael shook his head.

'You wait here, I'll speak to them first,' he said.

Phillippe gripped the steering wheel. He wanted to run to his family. He took out his phone and called them. He smiled and wiped a tear away. Nicola didn't notice. She had twisted her head round to watch Michael walk towards the building.

Michael walked up the staircase and was directed into a meeting room. Fifteen men were huddled around a table meant for twelve. They looked sombre. They were angry. Michael was surprised. This must be all of them he thought. They said nothing. The tall sombre man sat at one of the long edges of the table. He got up, offered Michael his seat and then stood beside him with folded arms. Thirty eyes were on him. Michael realised how dishevelled he looked.

'When my grandfather started this, he made a living running illegal booze, a good living,' Michael said.

'Do you have it?' one of the men said. Michael raised his hand. The man raised his eyebrows.

'When my father died, my mother took over and it was she who realised that all we had to do was control corporations, buy up enough stock, more or less legal, less dangerous. Until Klober came along and tried to take it all away. I've done some terrible things for this organisation, I know you don't think I'm man enough, I know my mother didn't think I was man enough. But I want to make amends, for everything that I have done.' Michael stood up and walked to the door. He closed it and locked it and put the key in his pocket.

'Could you draw the curtains please,' he said to no one in particular. The tall sombre man pulled the curtains shut. The dim lights of the room seemed almost like candlelight.

Michael sat back at the table. The air quickly felt stuffy and sour.

'I want to make amends,' he said again and he reached into his pocket. The fifteen men leant closer. Michael placed the object on the table, pulled the pin, and watched the lever ping across the room. It took a second for panic and then a scramble for the door and three and a half more before the panic was futile.

Nicola and Phillippe jumped out of their skins. The rumble echoed and cracked along the streets. Car alarms sounded, and fragments hit their car, some hard, some soft. Phillippe gathered his senses and drove away. Nicola stared out of the back window.

28

The cafe bustled. Traffic coursed nearby and people, lots of people. They seemed to detect the hint of spring. Nicola sat at an outside table, wrapped warm. Her coffee steamed. Phillippe appeared with a little girl. Nicola smiled.

'This is Claire,' Phillippe said. He smiled. He looked like he had good news, not an ounce of tension in his soul. He looked ten years younger.

'They are all gone,' he said. Deliberately cryptic in front of the little girl. Claire was drawing on a napkin. The waitress who brought her some crayons smiled at them.

'How old are you Claire?' Nicola said, holding Claire's free hand. The girl grinned, unable to answer, her daddy nudged her.

'Six,' she said.

'Not like you to have a bag,' Phillippe said.

'It's too big to fit in my pocket.' Nicola took the box from her bag and they looked at it. Claire oblivious, lost in her drawing.

'Why do you want to do this so bad? You have won,' Phillippe said. Nicola looked at the little girl, and

Phillippe saw that she couldn't answer in front of Claire.
Nicola put the box back in her bag.

'Do you know how to use it?' Phillippe said.

'I do.'

PART TWO

I

Hiding something like this was impossible. So, they opted to hide in plain sight. Years of experience showed that this was the best, the only way. Security, minimal. It would only attract attention. They even had occasional guided tours. They made components. Electronic components? Sort of, they would say. There are some trade secrets, despite the friendly, open nature of the business.

The woman observing them from the nearby hill wouldn't have bothered them. The land around the factory was open access. A wildlife reserve. Owned by the corporation, but given back to the people, and to nature. Solidarity to the world.

Nicola looked along the sleek copper roof, still shiny in places. She twisted the focus on the green part of the roof, made from turf with wildflowers and then along to the solar panels. That was where she noticed something odd.

She wondered who was running the factory. Where the mandate was for its existence. Who are its customers? It shouldn't still be here at all.

She looked again at the solar panels. Was she imagining it? She zoomed in. No. She wasn't.

Inside the factory a tour was in progress. The tour guide, a young woman, beautiful and articulate, addressed the assembled passengers. They rode in a small train, like a string of golf buggies. Each car emblazoned with the company logo. There were robot arms dancing with such choreographed precision, you would think it was an act for the spectators. It was. They lapped it up, looked at their host's perfect smile and bought it all. Why wouldn't they? The tour guide believed it was true and that truth she cast over her audience.

The real work went on deeper in the complex. Out of sight, almost fully automated and in an area that made up only a tenth of the factory. Lots of small CNC machines working on tiny little pieces of glass. Each machine placing a tiny Y shaped scratch on the tiny, flat pieces of glass. But it was the glass that was the real innovation. Almost indestructible and under the right conditions, it resonates at the perfect frequency.

Nicola continued to focus on the solar panels. Someone was up there amongst them. The figure moved about, zigzagging, half crouching. Whoever they were, they moved like an amateur, guided by Hollywood than by any real training. Their face covered by a balaclava, the figure stopped and awkwardly reached into a pocket. It hovered by one of the thick cables that came from a large junction box and then tried to gnaw at the cable with the implement. Probably wire cutters, wire cutters that weren't up to the job.

Nicola was feeling tense. She wished the figure would give up and go away. She relied on stealth, patience, observation. She relied on things humming along as normal. Nothing out of the ordinary. She knew she should have made a start a couple of days ago. She cursed herself.

Did that idiot have any idea what would happen if they cut through that cable? They would be blown off the roof, dead or half dead before they hit the ground. If hitting the ground didn't finish them off.

Nicola weighed her options. Give up and move on, maybe wait another year and come back, or try and stop this idiot from ruining everything. She hated to leave things half-finished and decided to find her way onto the roof.

She would have to hug the tree line round to the other side of the building, where the hillside was closest to the roof. It could take too long, but she would hear the electrical explosion, probably see the sparks. She could then call it a day and come back again in a year or so. Either way, she may as well try.

She hacked her way round, growing madder with every scratch. After what felt like hours, she found the spot that led onto the turf roof. The roof sloped back towards the hillside. She kept under the horizon of the roof and ran along towards the solar panels. She hadn't been up here yet and she was surprised by the size of the panels. They were like a giant pixel forest, cables running neatly like black vines. She went to the cusp of the roof so she could look across to the place on the hill she had been and orientated herself. She got down low and listened.

She heard the gnawing sound of the cutters. Whoever they were, they were determined. Nicola crawled under the panels and over the cables, following the sound.

She saw a pair of boot clad feet moving slightly. They were smaller than she expected, and she could now hear exasperated grunts and sighs. They sounded feminine. Nicola got as close as she could. The idiot was small, Nicola loomed over it and grabbed it around the arms and torso. It kicked and cried out, muffled by the balaclava.

'Shut up,' Nicola growled into its ear. She slid one hand over its mouth and dragged it back below the horizon of the roof and held tight.

'Shut up,' she said again. She held tighter until the squirming figure acquiesced. Nicola let go and looked into dark eyes that weren't afraid, but angry. She pulled off the balaclava to see the face of an olive skinned, dark haired girl of about twelve.

'Get off me,' the girl said.

'I just saved your life,' Nicola said.

'I don't need saving.'

'If you had got though that cable, you would be dead,' Nicola said.

'What would your people care,' the girl said.

'My people?'

'Your people.'

'I don't work here,' Nicola said.

The girl said nothing.

'How old are you?' Nicola said.

'Go fuck yourself and let go of me.'

Nicola smiled and let go of her.

'Why were you trying to cut through that cable?'

'I want to fuck this place up, that's why, what's it to you?'

Nicola smiled again.

'What's so funny, bitch?' the girl said. Nicola switched her smile to a hard stare.

'That's enough,' Nicola said. The girl glanced at the ground for a second before meeting Nicola's gaze again head on.

'I'm going now,' the girl said.

'Okay, want to tell me your name first?'

'No.'

The girl got up and walked away.

'What did you mean by *my people*?' Nicola said.

She turned her head to the side.

'Whiteskin,' she said and she looked ahead again and held up a middle finger.

Nicola took a look at the cable. The girl had hardly dented it. The wire cutters were on the junction box. They looked antique. Nicola put them in her pocket and made her way off the roof. She looked around to see if she could see the girl, but she had vanished.

2

That night activity in the factory was much the same. No one came up on the roof, so no one else had noticed anything. Nicola was using night vision. It brought to life roosting birds and the movement of various animals. Some big. All hungry. It was distracting, tiring. Potentially dangerous. So, she decided to pack up and go to a cheap hotel. She had been watching the place for weeks. Nothing ever happened at night. She was sure of that now. There was the chance that more activity occurred at different times of the year, but now, nothing was going to happen. She decided to take one last sweep with the night vision, then she would pack up for sure. As she swept her head round, the goggles picked up the animals again, but now there was something else. A human figure crawling on the roof, at the same spot, fumbling around. Nicola looked down and pressed her hand on her head. This girl was literally a headache.

Nicola had to hack the same route as before, except it was dark. By the time she got to the roof again she was boiling with rage. Confronting the girl was pointless. So, Nicola waited. She lay low on the turf roof and watched the luminescent footsteps under the panels. She waited until the footsteps gave up and walked onto the turf roof and almost walked over her. Nicola watched the girl cross from the roof onto the bank. She got up and fixed the night vision to her head and followed the ghostly image into the woods. Nicola kept well behind. Almost at the risk of losing her. She knew the girl was smart; inexperienced but far from stupid.

Nicola followed her out of the woods the far side of the hill and onto a track. The track was loose gravel, crunchy under foot, noisy. She kept to a tyre rut, compact, quiet, but awkward. The girl in front walked calmly. Her footsteps crunching. Nicola followed her for about two miles. The girl got to the entrance of a property and went through it without looking back. Nicola got to the entrance and kept low behind a scrubby hedge. Down a wide, unkempt driveway was a small, timber framed house with a veranda and weatherboarding. Nicola took off her night vision and sat for a while to let her eyes adjust. She made sure the strap around her neck was secure and tucked them under her jacket. They pressed uncomfortably into her breasts. Her vision recovered and she felt unencumbered and free to turn her head and feel the air around. She looked at the house again, now silhouetted by a faint moon glow and she felt an oppressive, grey sadness.

Nicola, still keeping low, crept along the edge of the path, keeping to the grassy edge, her footsteps soft. She crept up to the low veranda, and bit down on her lip, willing it not to creak. Then she felt the barrel of a gun press into the nape of her neck.

'What are you doing here bitch?'

'I brought you something,' Nicola said.

'Put your hands up.'

'No.'

'Put them up now or I'll blow your head off.'

'Fine, do it.'

'I – I mean it.'

Nicola moved her head to the side fast, span on one foot, grabbed the barrel of the shotgun and kicked the girl to the ground. Nicola stood over her, holding the shotgun by the barrel. The girl's dark eyes glistened in the faint moonlight. She held her ribs and started to groan. Nicola snapped open the breach of the gun and put the two cartridges into her pocket. She offered a hand to the girl. She reluctantly took it. The girl's eyes glistened even more with pregnant tears.

'You going to stop all this shit?' Nicola said.

'Who are you lady . . . why you following me?'

'Nicola reached into her pocket and gave the girl the wire cutters.'

The girl snatched them from her, a tear fell down her cheek.

'Are your parents in?'

'They're asleep, you better get out of here, you'll be sorry if you wake them up.'

'I want to talk to them,' Nicola said.

'You can't, they're sleeping.'

'Then I will come back tomorrow.'

The girl said nothing.

'I will be here at eight in the morning,' Nicola said.

'I won't be here.'

'You will, and you will stay off that roof.' Nicola handed the shotgun back to the girl.

'You stay off that roof. Tomorrow morning, we will introduce ourselves properly, you understand?'

'Yes.'

'You understand?'

'Yes.'

Nicola walked out of the drive and up the track. She didn't look back. She walked on, not knowing where the track would lead. All of her focus was on the factory. She was blind to everything else. This was a welcome diversion. She followed the track and her instincts, turning where she thought it was right to do so. Eventually she came to the nearby town. Its few lights glittering, and she found a small motel by the main road. It was an old building, run down, C shaped with parking within the embrace of the C. It had two floors, outside stairs to outside balconies. It had a couple of cars in the carpark and a half-broken neon sign that said there was a twenty-four-hour reception. She found the door to the reception. There sat an old man, half asleep, a forty-year-old TV crackled with some old show. It was plumbed into an equally old VCR. The old man nearly fell off his chair when he saw Nicola. He straightened his cap.

'Can I help you miss?'

'I need a room.'

'Take your pick, ground floor or first floor?'

'First floor please.'

The man hovered his hand over the racks of keys, seeming to play a rhythm in his mind, and picked a key from the middle of the first rack.

'This is probably the cleanest,' he said.

'Thanks, what do I owe you?'

'I'd see the room first and then ask me what I owe you,' he said and then laughed before breaking into a coughing fit. He waved Nicola away and went out back, the coughing worsened. He disappeared behind a door.

Nicola frowned, put the folded bills back in her pocket and crossed the carpark to the nearest staircase. She walked with great care. The staircase was made from buckled, rusting steel and was a lawsuit waiting to happen. One of the rooms had old police tape across the door, old and faded. Breached long ago, the tape flapped. Nicola found her room, double checked the number and struggled with the lock. Eventually she got into the room. It wasn't as bad as she had expected. It was dusty, musty and hadn't been used for maybe a couple of years. Mould grew on peeling wallpaper that went out of fashion in nineteen seventy-four. Nicola got out her phone, switched it on, set it for six AM. She took off her pack and took the night vision goggles from around her neck, stuffing them in the pack. She took off her boots and lay back fully clothed on the bed. She fell asleep quickly, the few hours she would get in a proper bed would be worth it.

The alarm startled Nicola from a deep, dreamless sleep. She looked at the light through the threadbare curtains, double checked the time and went to the bathroom. She put on her pack and left the room to the crisp, bright morning. The hotel balcony had quite a view. She hadn't been able to cast her eyes over a vista for a while. Beyond the telephone and power cables, the low rooftops and wide, spartan roads was Montana.

*   *   *

Nicola made the dangerous descent down the staircase and walked over to the reception. The door creaked open and the same old man walked up to the desk. Same clothes, same crackling TV.

'Do you have a car I can rent?' she said.

'Sure,' he said and rummaged in a drawer. He took out a key.

'The Civic out there, that's probably the most reliable.'

Nicola took the key.

'I guess this goes on my account?' Nicola said.

'Sure, if it don't have much gas, there's the gas station out left, just down the street,' he said.

'Thanks.' Nicola went over to the Civic. The other car in the carpark was an old Buick Century sedan. Tyres flat, mouldy, the bodywork bleached a sallow tan with rust framing every panel.

Nicola opened the door to the Civic and tossed her pack onto the back seat. The car was tatty, smelt a little funny, but it started. Nicola had to slide the seat back. Probably the owner's car, she thought. The engine ran lumpy. She put it in drive and then checked the fuel gauge. Quarter tank, ok for now. It was unlikely the gas station was open yet anyway. She doubted if the old man at the motel had any concept of time. She turned out left down the wide street. Only a couple of cars drove by opposite, both drivers waved and then looked with surprise to see a driver they didn't recognise. She drove past the Googie style gas station. Its sign like a rocket ship. It was shut. The town began to fade away and Nicola found the track she had walked up a few hours before. Pale gold gravel. The suspension had seen better days. It would have been more comfortable to walk. Tracking her way back through her memory, she found the crossroads and junctions. She was at the old house by seven. It was quiet, no lights, no sound. She pulled the forty-year-old Civic down into the sloping drive, crushing grass and fledgling shrubs, and switched off the engine.

The house looked neglected. She could see it now in the dawn light. Lower than the road, half hidden. An old buffalo skin hung up near the door. There were a couple of old easy chairs on the veranda. Weeds came up through the boards. She couldn't feel the presence of another soul. Her boots clapped firmly on the boards of the porch and she pulled the flyscreen open and tried the door handle. It was locked. Nicola stood back, let the fly screen close hard. She stood to one side of the door. Waited. Nothing. She walked around the house, struggling through thick prairie grass. All the windows were either boarded shut on the outside or closed off with blinds on the inside. All the windows were fastened shut.

There were outbuildings, paths to them neglected. Wrecked cars in some. Junk and old tools in the rest. But there was a hint of recent life in the place. There were no other buildings for miles around. None habitable. Nicola was sure that the girl was here or had been recently. She walked back up to the front door and knocked hard. No answer.

Nicola heard the faint growl of a V8 and the crunch of tyres getting louder. She stepped back off the porch and walked to get a clear view up the drive. A brand-new Chevy pickup pulled up and blocked the way out. Black gloss paint, dusted. It had a crew cab. Its windows blackened. It sat there, its dust cloud overtook it and faded, the engine stopped, then all four doors opened.

3

Nicola sat on the hood of the Civic and folded her arms. Four men got out of the truck and lined up along the entrance of the drive. One tall, wearing a black shirt, one shorter and a lot fatter. The other two average size, athletic. The rest of them wearing check shirts. All of them wearing jeans and boots. The tall one in the black shirt was the driver. He was older than the others. Forties. The others mid-thirties. They smiled politely. The tall one in the black shirt spoke.

'You okay Miss?'

'I'm fine. Thanks for asking.' Nicola unfolded her arms, held her thighs. Smiled. The men all cast their eyes over her.

'That car ain't built for these old tracks,' he said.

'Wanna swap?' Nicola said.

The men broke out in a little chuckle. The two average sized men hung their thumbs in their belt loops. Probably brothers, Nicola thought.

The fat one was silent. The tall, older one spoke again.

'That 'ol Cyril's car?'

'The man at the Motel?' Nicola said.

'That's him. He lend it to you?'

'I hired it.'

There was an awkward silence.

'What you doing out here Miss?' the tall man said.

'Nature watching.'

The tall man rubbed his forehead, looked up and smiled at Nicola.

'Why you on this property?' he said.

The other men were looking a little stony faced.

'The car was running bad. Was looking for help,' Nicola said.

'Little early to be knocking on folks' doors?'

'I thought country folk were always up early?'

The tall man stared at her hard. Nicola folded her arms again.

'Perhaps we can take a look. Wanna pop the hood?'

'Shouldn't we let these people know first, what we're all doing on their property?' she said.

'No one lives here.' The fat man spoke. The others looked at him. He looked down and swallowed. They all turned their eyes again on Nicola.

'Kinda looks like someone lives here,' Nicola said. She looked back at the house and cast her eyes around. She met the gaze of the tall man again.

'No one has lived here for months,' the tall man said. Nicola stood up. The near useless suspension of the Civic sprung the car up six inches.

'I think the shocks are shot,' the tall man said. Nicola walked up to the men. She was taller than three of them and only an inch shorter than the older man. She walked to the other side of the truck and ran her fingers through the dust on the paintwork. The taller man got a little agitated.

'Don't do that! You'll scratch it,' he said. Nicola looked across at him over the back of the truck. The men huddled, off guard, out of position, out of character.

'Anywhere I can hire a truck like this?' Nicola said.

'This is the only one in town,' the tall man said, he nodded to the fat man, who walked down the drive to the Civic, opened the driver's door and then popped the hood. Nicola craned her neck to see around the tall man's shoulder.

'Rick here will know what to do,' he said. Rick started the engine. It ran okay. Rick shut the hood, looked around the car and took Nicola's pack from the back seat. He left the engine running. He walked up to the tall man and handed him the pack.

'Mind if we take a look in your bag?' the tall man said.

'I do.'

The tall man gave Rick a nod. He began to undo the straps on top of the pack. Nicola held her hand up, palm out. This stopped him. They all looked at her.

'I said. I do mind.'

Rick started to unloop the strap again. Nicola walked around the truck, running her finger in the dust. She pushed past the two shorter men and gripped the bag. The old Civic engine was still running.

'You the local law?' Nicola said. The tall man laughed. The others chuckled. Nicola leant back on the truck.

147

They formed an arc around her. She gripped the bag harder and pulled it. Rick pulled back. A tug of war.

'Let go of the bag Rick,' she said. Rick smiled and tugged hard, the bag ripped slightly, Nicola let go of the bag and Rick fell backwards. His back hit the dust. Small rocks dug in. He groaned. Nicola walked forward. Grabbed the bag off him. The other men looked to the tall man. Nicola walked to the Civic, opened the door and tossed the bag back on the back seat. She looked back at the men. They pulled Rick up and dusted him down and laughed at him. The tall man smiled and walked down the slope towards Nicola.

'We need to know what you are doing around here,' he said.

'You need to get that truck out the way,' Nicola said.

One of the 'brothers' opened the door of the Chevy. He got out a revolver. Nicola narrowed her eyes and looked hard. It looked like a .357. The tall man followed her gaze and looked at him. They all smiled again. He looked back at Nicola.

'Are you all that scared of me?' she said. She laughed, throwing her head back.

'What can I do?' Nicola said and she turned to the side and waved an inviting arm towards the door of the Civic. The tall man patted Nicola on the shoulder, opened the door and leant in.

Nicola looked at the driver's seat, tempted to jump in and floor it towards the truck. She ran it through her head. Jump in, seatbelt (important), put it in drive, handbrake off. Then what? Too many steps, too much risk. She stood by. The engine running. She let the man get back out of the car with the bag.

She walked past him, brushing a breast on his arm and stood so that he was between her and his men. He turned his back to his men to face her.

She put her hands on his as he held the top of the pack.

'I still can't let you look inside,' she said.

Nicola looked over his shoulder. He blocked the line of sight between her and the gun man. She gripped his hands a little tighter, leant back and rammed her fore-head into the bridge of his nose. He spluttered and stumbled. His men ran forward. The gun man fumbled. She let go of the tall man's hands and rammed her forehead into his face again. He was down and barely conscious. She wiped most of the blood off her face with her sleeve. She stood back. The fat man, Rick, was the first to reach her. This was a surprise. He tripped over the tall man and as he did the other two grabbed her by the arms. She looked up. The .357 was on the ground near the Chevy. Nicola stamped into the small of the fat man's back. He screamed, something broke. The other two still held her arms. She kicked the one to her left in the groin. He doubled up. She punched the other one in the eye and ran to the gun. She checked it. It was loaded. She pulled back the hammer. The man with the swollen eye was still standing, only just.

'Pass me my bag,' she said.

He tossed it towards her. The engine of the Civic was still running. She looked in the Chevy. The keys were in the ignition. She fired a round at the standing man's feet. She started the engine and kicked up gravel and spun the truck in the opposite direction. Nicola headed back towards the town.

The Chevy almost glided over the track. She slid it round the junctions and crossroads. She floored it as hard as she could. She cursed herself for spending too long looking at the factory. She was out in the open now. There was no coming back here next year, or for years afterwards.

Nicola couldn't get the girl out of her mind. She tore up the main road and into the carpark of the Motel. The old man was standing at the door to his office, his jaw dropped when he saw Nicola get out of the Chevy.

'Cyril?' she said. She grabbed her bag and walked over to the old man. Cyril nodded. 'Your car will be back in a minute.' She handed him the keys to the pickup. 'I'll be staying a little longer.' She walked across to the steel steps. 'I'm Nicola, by the way.'

Nicola went to her room. Threw down the bag, washed herself up and lay on the bed. She was hungry.

4

It took half an hour for the Civic to turn up. By that time Nicola had grown impatient and found a diner. She ordered a big breakfast, had lots of coffee and ignored the sideways glances and whispers.

She had a window seat, looked out at the wide road, its black surface crazed by harsh winters and scorching heat. Today was mild, a good spring day. The views were good across the low horizon. The sky was big, endless. She wondered how anyone made a living in this place. The black Chevy pickup pulled up on the street. The two brothers got out. One of them couldn't walk so fast. The other one had a neat, white patch covering an eye. They saw her through the window. Nicola hurried up her eating.

One eye marched through the door. The door swung back and hit his much slower brother in the face. One eye marched towards Nicola, followed eventually by his brother. They hovered over her table. Nicola held up her index finger as One eye was about to speak. She held the finger up until had she finished eating and then drained her coffee cup. A big woman came over and poured her another coffee.

'No trouble in here,' she mumbled to One eye.

'What do you want?' Nicola said.

'Rick may never walk again,' One eye said.

'Then he should have minded his own business.'

One eye leant forward and raised his fist. Nicola reached under the table and pulled out the .357 revolver. They both stood back.

Nicola stood up. The brothers backed off. She tucked the gun away.

'The bills on them,' Nicola said to the big woman and she walked out of the diner and back to the Motel.

Cyril sat in his office. The TV wasn't on. He looked afraid.

'You'd better get out of here,' he said. He glanced out the window. Nicola followed his gaze. He looked up at the door with the old police tape. Nicola understood.

'Not yet,' she said. Nicola wanted to see if Cyril was fine. He was fine enough.

'I want to know about the room with the police tape,' she said.

'Some out of town drifter, died of an overdose,' Cyril said.

'Can I take a look?'

Cyril said nothing for a few seconds, inhaled deeply, shook his head and handed Nicola the key.

'There's nothing in there,' he said.

Nicola took the key and walked up the dangerous steps. The door was difficult to unlock. Stale air and half-darkness exhaled from the room as the door opened. The light didn't work. She pulled open the drapes and coughed with the dust. The room was the same as hers. The bed was just a frame. No mattress. The drawers of the side table were open. A Gideon bible in one of the drawers. In the bathroom the outlet pipes had been taken apart and the toilet cistern had been removed. A mirrored cabinet, open, empty. Nicola caught her reflection in the mottled glass.

She went back to the bedroom and made her way to the door when something caught her eye. She looked down by the bed post and found an earring. A bead of some kind. Deep, smoky orange. She held it in her hand and put it in her pocket and went back out.

As she locked the door a black Chevy pickup pulled up outside the reception. Exactly like the one before, darkened windows, except emblazoned with the word SHERIFF. Nicola paused, looked down at it. The .357 was tucked in her waist. Nicola leant on the railing. The door of the pickup opened and out got a powerfully built woman. She put on her hat and checked her radio and looked up at Nicola. She folded her arms and waited for Nicola to walk down the steps. The two women nodded an acknowledgement at each other.

'I'm going to need to take possession of that revolver Miss,' she said.

Nicola lifted her shirt, revealing the gun. The Deputy took it, checked it and tossed it on the driver's seat of the pickup. Cyril hovered in the doorway. He scratched his head under his cap.

'I didn't call her,' he said.

'I know you didn't,' Nicola said, her eyes fixed on the Deputy.

'I need to see some identification,' the deputy said.

Nicola looked at the name badge on her vest. Novak.

'It's in my room,' Nicola said. 'Okay if I go get it?'

Novak nodded. Nicola walked across to the steel steps and went up to her room. Her bag was gone. Her jeans from yesterday were gone. She had left her driving license in them. Stupid. This is what happens when you go off plan, she thought.

Nicola clenched her fists and bit on her bottom lip. She took some deep breaths to calm down. Closed the door to the room and went back down the steps. Cyril couldn't meet her stare. His eyes said 'sorry'.

Nicola said nothing. Novak twitched a little smile from the corner of her mouth and opened the rear door of the crew cab. She took out Nicola's backpack and gave it to her. She got back in the pickup and drove away.

Cyril shut himself in his office. Nicola went back up to her room. Everything was in the bag except her night goggles and binoculars. Spare clothes, hygiene stuff, an envelope.

She opened the envelope. It had her driver's license, a bus timetable and a note.

It said 'GO'.

Nicola took the bag, had a quick look around the room and put the driver's licence in her pocket. She went back down to the reception. Cyril looked at her with cowed eyes.

'What do I owe you?' she said.

'Nothing.'

Nicola nodded at him and walked down the main street. She went into the diner. There were no customers. The big woman didn't speak. Nicola bought a large bottle of water and some food to take away. She left the bus timetable on the counter. She walked out of town and headed for the house. The walk seemed longer this time. Halfway there she saw a thick column of smoke rise in the distance. She upped her pace, got to the house, it was burning, had been for a while. The flames were past their zenith and a tangled mass of charred lumber fuelled the remaining flames. The outbuildings had burnt and smouldered. The prairie grass had charred and smouldered at the boundary of the flames. The ground was still wet enough to stop a prairie fire, hopefully. Nicola sat at the edge of the drive, drank some of the water and ate some of the food. If only she had wrapped things up a few days ago.

Her thoughts of dejection were broken by the sound of a light aircraft approaching, any immediate cover had burnt, or was on fire. Nowhere to hide.

The factory was two miles away. She would be seen by the airplane no matter what she did. She walked on and cast her eyes over the burning wreck of someone's home. Nicola reached into her pocket and looked at the earring. She looked back at the house and put the earring back into her pocket and walked up the gravel road. The plane buzzed overhead, following the path of the road. Nicola felt the eyes of the pilot on her, she felt more than one person was in the plane. The sky was too bright to get a good look at it. She could only see its silhouette. A dark, slow dot against an endless sky. It faded away to the east.

An hour later, Nicola was in position overlooking the factory. It felt like home, the past thirty-six hours seemed like an abstract dream. She only had her naked eyeballs now. She saw no trace of the figure on the roof. The girl was the only thing she was looking out for.

What she did see was the black Chevy pull up by the loading bay. The tall man with the black shirt got out. His nose heavily bandaged. It was hard to see, it was distant. He walked into the loading bay. Nicola craned forward, desperate to close the distance. The thick loading bay doors stayed open. She stashed her pack in the undergrowth and made her way, cat-like, down to the factory.

Nicola stopped at the edge of the blacktop surface. Just out of sight. She could see the pickup clearly, see a little way inside the loading bay. She could make out the muffled sound of conversation and then a scream, high pitched. The tall man with the black shirt carried the girl over his shoulder. She was unconscious. Nicola hoped she was just unconscious. He slid the cover back and threw her in the back of the pickup and slid the cover over and locked it in place. His eyes were red and the flesh around them puffy, turning black. The dressing on his nose was stained and mottled brown with blood. The loading bay doors closed as the tall man got into the driver's seat, closed the door and started the engine. He pulled away quick.

Nicola headed over a small embankment and then up to higher ground. She saw the pickup leave the drive and turn onto the main road towards town. She watched the pickup grow distant. Her eyes burned at the object as it went away. The factory was built within a small island of hills in the middle of the prairie. Only the soft undulation of the land hid the distant vehicle from view. Nicola couldn't bear to take her eyes from the spot, willing the pickup to appear again, but it didn't.

As she turned her head, something caught her eye. She turned back and saw a distant plume of dust rise. He had turned off the blacktop. She knew where.

5

Nicola had scoured maps and aerial images of the area for months before she had arrived. She had committed them to memory. She thought back to when she had spotted the house, now cinders, and thought nothing of it. There were houses much the same all around, outbuildings, remains; built at a time when the surrounding population was twice the size it is now. Nicola knew the track the Chevy had turned up. She only knew from maps and images from high above. She wasn't familiar with the final details. The track was on the periphery of her focus, but she knew it. She wished she could fly the vast distance. It seemed nearer than it really was in the open landscape. The girl could be dead. Probably was dead. But she could be alive. Nicola turned her gaze along the stretch of asphalt that ran dart straight through the prairie with its subtle vertical undulations. Riding over it like a dark fleck, a vehicle appeared on the horizon. It headed towards the dirt road.

The dust cloud lingered and rose in distant, dispersing puffs and the fate of the girl darkened. Nicola might just make it to the road, she might just catch that distant vehicle. She made her way to the road as fast as she could.

Not caring about being in the open, or being seen, she got to the driveway and ran along it.

The vehicle neared and it was an old, square grilled Dodge Ram. Nicola waved at it. A gesture way beyond the simple thumb of a hitch hiker. Nicola would only rarely try and stop a car by the side of the road. It felt too much like having to rely on outside forces. When she did hitchhike though, nearly all the time the first car or truck would stop for her.

The old pickup slowed and then stopped. It was driven by a young boy of about sixteen. Nicola jumped in before being invited.

'Drive fast to the crossroads,' she said.

'Uh – sure,' the boy said. Nicola was panting. The boy could hardly keep his eyes off her.

'Eyes on the road,' she said.

The boy gulped and put his foot harder on the gas.

They made it to the crossroads.

'Turn left,' she said.

The boy stopped the truck.

'I can't,' he said. Nicola stared hard at the boy. He flinched. 'I can't go down there.'

The dirt track crossed the asphalt and stretched to the horizon either side.

'I need you to turn left,' she said.

'You're gonna have to get out Miss.'

'I'm sorry,' Nicola said and she punched him quickly at the side of the neck. The boy didn't flinch, didn't see it coming. He was unconscious.

Nicola dragged him out of the truck. The engine was still running. She found a bag in the back, put it at the side of the crossroads and laid the boy on his side and used the bag as a pillow. She checked him. He was breathing and starting to groan. She found a bottle of water in the cab and put it in front of him. She jumped back in the pickup and floored it down the dirt track. She felt a little ashamed, then even more so, when she realised the boy was now in a thick cloud of dust.

The Dodge flew along the track that seemed to go on for ever, but then came to an abrupt end. A small googie style building was in front of her. Crumbling, faded. Shaped like the tailfin of a fifties automobile. The half-demolished remains of a control tower nearby. Collapsed silos in the distance. There was a runway of no more than mown prairie grass. A tractor off to the side of it with a mower attached. A light aircraft parked at the end of the runway; fuel cans next to it and the pilot's door ajar. The black Chevy pickup parked beside the plane. Nicola walked up to the Chevy, instinctively crouching low. The cover to the back was open. No sign of the girl. A trace of blood.

Nicola heard the noise of crashing, gunshots and shouts from inside the building. But they weren't real, more like a movie, but they were disjointed. Nicola checked in the back of the pickup for any weapons. There were none, only a wheel wrench, so she took it and walked up to the door, placing her ear against it. She could hear voices in the maelstrom of noise. Real human voices, laughing, arguing. They were male.

Nicola turned the door handle and the door popped open. The noise was almost deafening, and it sounded like a computer game. She was in a wide corridor. A window to the runway at the opposite end thirty feet away. There were four doors, two either side of the corridor. She tried to concentrate over the abrupt yells coming from the first door on the right. The wheel wrench poised above her head. She gripped the handle of the door to the left. She would leave the noisy room till last. She turned the handle slowly, feeling every twitch in the mechanism.

She now held the wheel wrench behind her back. She could use one hand to defend, and bring the wrench up from behind, striking under the jaw if she needed to.

Fresh air hit her nostrils. The room was heavily dusted with the golden dust from outside. The dust entered through a broken window. There were rows of seats, an old waiting room. On the seats were pieces of junk that looked like old plane parts. The remains of old posters were on the walls, illegible. Ceiling tiles missing, an old light fitting hung down with no bulb. Nicola cast her eyes around. The room didn't have the feel of life, she may have been the first person to open the door in years. She closed the door slow and quiet, though it didn't matter; the noise of the shoot 'em up computer game reverberated. Whoever was playing it must be half deaf. She got the idea that two men were in there. Probably the brothers. Half blind, half crippled, unable to hear anything. Stupid. The noise of the video game confused her senses. The old part of her brain half registering the gunshots and shouts as real. It was making her very angry.

She knew there was a third man somewhere. The tall guy in the black shirt. He too was compromised, but more able than the others. Nicola went to the far door on the left. The room next to the old waiting room. She repeated the procedure, turned the handle slowly, held the wheel wrench behind her back. A slither of pitch black and stale air. She could feel the presence of some-one in this room. She pushed the door open wider and heard a muffled gasp come from deep in the darkness. She opened the door wider casting a shaft of light into the room. In the corner of the room, two glistening dark eyes looked back at her. She was alive. The girl was bound and gagged with an old towel. She looked at Nicola with terror. Nicola held her finger to her lips. She looked around and mouthed 'anyone else in here?' The girl shook her head. Nicola crept into the room and untied the girl. She went to take off the gag when the girl's eyes widened and looked towards the door.

6

Nicola had got it wrong. Either more people had turned up, or more people were in there already. The tall guy with the black shirt was there, but he seemed subordinate now. Two other big fellas were in front of him, leaning round the door frame. The noise of the video game continued. It wasn't louder. Whoever was playing it didn't know of this situation. The door to their room hadn't been opened.

The two big fellas were well dressed. They looked tough, powerfully built. One had short sleeves; his fore-arm cut like a bodybuilder. He had a gold chain on his wrist. They were well groomed. Their brutish hands were manicured. They were drenched in cologne and looked a little sweaty. The tall guy behind them gulped.

'Two for one?' the man with the gold chain said. He laughed.

'She's too old,' the other one said, 'not worth the feed bill, he doesn't like blondes anyway.'

'I do,' the man with the chain said, 'she's good enough for me.'

Nicola still crouched over the girl. She probably looked like a captive, or they thought she was one of the abductors. The men were probably being sarcastic, about Nicola anyway. They sounded like they were from the East coast, probably New York. Nicola wasn't an expert on American accents.

The wheel wrench was on the floor beside her. There was an awkward, confused silence, only the third man behind knew what was going on. He started to sweat, but Nicola could see that he was more afraid of these men than he was of her. She stood up, deciding to leave the wheel wrench on the floor. She faced the men and took two steps forward. She said nothing.

They obviously thought she was part of it all.

'You messed up her head,' Nicola said to the tall man with the black shirt. He said nothing, looked like he couldn't find the words. Though behind the nose bandage and blackening eyes, it was hard to tell.

'What?' the man with the chain on his wrist said. 'We need them pure, untainted.' He came through the door, barging the other man out the way. He had a metal briefcase chained to his wrist. Nicola stepped out of the way and he pulled the girl up by the arm. The untied ropes fell to the ground as he yanked her arm up. The big man frowned.

'What's going on?' he said. He bent down and picked up the rope. The girl trembled and her eyes looked liquid, Nicola looked into them and smiled. The girl started to hyperventilate. Nicola took off the gag. The girl was silent.

The man next to Nicola was big. He was a killer; she could see it in him. He was tough. A good punch might not work, then she would be overwhelmed. She couldn't pick up the wheel wrench before. They would have backed away, put themselves in a better position. They were more than likely armed. They would shoot her. It would be a mess and Nicola would be the mess. She bent down, brushed her shoulder on the man's leg. He didn't get a chance to react as she came back up fast and smashed the wrench into his jaw. She felt the crunch of his teeth breaking and his jaw snap. He went over backwards, hit his head on the wall, but got straight back up. He reached behind him. A gun.

The other man came forward. Nicola grabbed him and pushed him into the man with the briefcase. They crumpled backwards into the wall. Nicola had dropped the wheel wrench. The tall man was shouting, trying to get help, but the others couldn't hear. The girl had gone. Nicola ran at the tall man. She punched him in the throat. He went down. She was in the corridor, she saw the front door swing shut. Nicola ran for it. She was grabbed around the legs and she came crashing to the floor. She hit her head, her vision seemed to judder and her ears rang, but she was still alert. She tried to claw her way to the door when a pair of big feet in leather shoes appeared before her. She heard the click of a revolver hammer above the noise of the video game.

They pulled her up and gripping her upper arms they pushed her against the wall. The man with the broken jaw looked grotesque. The tall man was behind them, clutching his throat. He went into the room opposite, the noise of the video game became so loud, one of the men holding Nicola winced. The noise stopped. The brothers appeared, the one with the patch first, followed by the one who looked like he'd spent the night riding a horse. They looked shocked. The men holding Nicola looked at the other men, observing their injuries. They must have wondered how they could be dealing with such amateurs. Nicola's ears rang faintly.

The tall man in the black shirt tried to speak. But it was too hard. His throat was smashed. Nicola wished she had hit him harder. She looked down. The revolver was level with her belly. The big man pushed it hard against her stomach.

'What the hell is going on?' he said.

Nicola said nothing and smiled. He raised the revolver to her head. She could see the bare lead of the bullets in the chambers. The revolver was a snub nosed .38, chrome, highly polished. Nicola was taller than the men who held her. It was awkward holding the gun up to her head. The man holding it wheezed. Steroids getting to his heart, Nicola thought.

She looked up into the polished chrome of the gun. Blurred, out of focus. He held the gun steadier and pushed it harder into Nicola's forehead.

'Talk,' he said.

The man with the broken jaw tried to speak, but it was impossible. Nicola smiled and the man with the broken jaw gripped her arm harder. He raised his fist, the brief-case still attached to his wrist.

Nicola saw something reflect in the chrome of the gun. Then she heard the click of another revolver hammer. Everyone turned to face the direction it came from. The girl stood there, she was shaking and aiming a .357 magnum at the big man holding the .38.

Nicola was afraid. She was sure the girl was going to die. She focused on the girl's trembling finger on the trigger of the heavy gun. She had thought she would never see the girl again. Her feelings were mixed, but the distraction provided opportunity.

Nicola raised her knee hard into the groin of the man with the broken jaw. He crumpled, loosened the grip on her arm and she swept her elbow into the remains of his jaw. She continued the movement, bringing her fist into the other man's ear, just as he was turning his head back in her direction. At the same time, she moved her head to the side, away from the muzzle of the .38, and turned to look at the girl. Nicola reached for her. The tall man and the brothers piled into Nicola and the big men made a grab for her legs. She tumbled, clutching at air, she shouted, 'Run,' to the girl as she fell. Nicola was swamped in a confusion of arms and fists, of sweat and blood and cologne. She felt herself being pulled to the ground, she lost sight of the girl. A gunshot blasted.

7

'Get off her . . . NOW!' the girl shouted. The maelstrom of arms and legs stopped. Nicola climbed free. The tall man with the black shirt was down and clutched his right thigh. Deep red blood oozed from it. His thigh looked slightly bent. The femur shattered. He was dying and he knew it. His breaths were getting rapid. Nicola climbed out of the pile and walked over to the girl. She was trembling. Nicola held out her hand and took the gun from her without taking her eyes off the others. She held the pistol towards them and with her eyes fixed on them, she fumbled for the door handle to the old waiting room.

'Go in there. I promise I will get you. Put your hands over your ears.' She shut the door.

Nicola shot the two big men in the head. She shot the one with the broken jaw last. The brothers backed away. They put their hands up. Nicola sized them up and shot the one she had kicked in the balls earlier. The round slammed through the middle of his chest.

'Strip to your underpants,' she told One eye. He did. It was the most efficient way of making sure he was unarmed.

The door latch clicked.

'Stay in there!' Nicola shouted, but the girl ignored her. She held Nicola's hand.

'I've seen worse, don't worry about me,' she said.

'Go back in there and see if you can find that rope,' Nicola said. She nodded to the far room where the girl had been held. The girl got the rope.

'Tie 'ol One eye up, hands and feet. Hands behind his back,' Nicola said. The girl had seen everything. Nicola thought it best to distract her. She made an expert job of tying him up.

'Are you okay?' Nicola said. The girl nodded. 'Sorry you have to see this.'

The girl walked over to the man who had been shot in the leg and drove her heel into his wound. He woke from semi-consciousness and screamed.

'I'm okay with it,' the girl said and she checked him for weapons without Nicola asking. The girl found a knife and put it in her belt.

'Did they do anything to you?' Nicola said.

'We did nothing, nothing,' One eye shouted. 'We did nothing.'

The girl said nothing. She walked over to him and spat in his face and then kicked him in the stomach.

'Where did you find this?' Nicola said, gesturing with the gun.

'Glove compartment of the truck, why didn't you look there?'

'Didn't want to set off an alarm.'

'No one has car alarms here, they don't even lock their cars.'

Nicola scanned her eyes over the heaps of human flesh.

'Crime free zone,' she said and then she turned her attention to the tall man with the black shirt. A pool of dark blood grew around his leg and he was pale. He could barely talk, he was going to die. Nicola went to One eye, heaped up and bound against the wall. Nicola noticed a small tattoo that looked like Thor's hammer on his pasty, hairy chest. She looked again at his eye patch and ripped it off. The eye was puffed up with stitches in a couple of places.

'Anyone else in here?' Nicola said.

He shook his head.

'Anyone coming?' she said.

He shook his head again. Nicola opened the door to the games room. It stank of stale beer, fried food and cigarettes. A dump.

She dragged him by his hair into the room. 'Keep an eye on him,' she said to the girl. Nicola fished the .38 out from under one of the big guys and passed it to the girl. She checked it expertly and pointed it at the bound man.

The room was dingy. Two old couches, strewn with beer cans and bottles formed in an L shape. A small table in front with two overflowing ashtrays. The games console and TV, paused on a shoot 'em up game. A fridge, a microwave.

A connecting door led into the other room. Nicola cocked the hammer of the .357 and opened it.

Four leather chairs facing inward, a smartphone on a tripod, a laptop and a creepy box full of little girl's dresses. Nicola wanted to throw up. There was another door that led out to the corridor. She opened it, went into the corridor and shot the tall man in the chest. The girl came out of the room and pointed the .38.

'It's okay,' Nicola said and she followed the girl back into the room.

She bent down to One eye and pushed her thumb into his wounded eye. He screamed. The girl looked away. Nicola no longer cared about what she saw.

'Tell me everything,' she said and she pushed harder. The stitches began to break.

The girl began to wretch. She looked ill.

'Go get that smartphone in the other room,' Nicola said. The girl was happy to go. 'Don't switch it on.' The girl offered it to Nicola. 'Keep hold of it. Search the others for anything useful, empty their pockets and put it all somewhere safe.' The girl did as she was told.

Nicola's thumb was still pressed in the man's eye socket. His screams had become silent, as if they had run out. She withdrew her thumb, the impression remained, slowly rebounding.

'Look through the clothes this one took off too,' Nicola shouted. A weak 'OK' came from the girl. 'Stay out there,' Nicola called. The girl was happy to oblige this time. The man started to mumble. Nicola slapped him hard across his face.

'Talk,' she said. She wiped her thumb on the arm of the couch. He whimpered again, she slapped him harder.

'We—we only did it a couple of times,' he said. His nose streamed, mucus ran into his mouth and stretched between his lips as he spoke.

'Not about that, about the factory,' Nicola said.

8

'I don't know anything. Doug knew about it all.'

'Doug?'

'The tall guy.'

'So, you are telling me you're no use to me?' Nicola said.

'No—No . . .' Nicola shot him in the stomach.

'I'm sorry,' the girl said. She was shaking and crying.

'I'm sorry you had to go through all this,' Nicola said and she wrapped her arms around the girl. The girl squeezed Nicola hard and let out a muffled wail. Nicola tapped her on the back.

'We need to get out of here,' Nicola said.

The girl nodded, Nicola wiped away the girl's tears.

Nicola cast her eyes around and then searched the rooms for anything of use. She looked in the fridge, under the couches, everywhere. She set the girl to help.

'Do you have all that stuff from their pockets?'

'Yes, and I found these.' The girl had Nicola's binoculars and night vision goggles. Nicola smiled.

She cast her eyes around again.

'One more thing,' Nicola said. She went over to the metal briefcase, still attached to an arm.

'Any keys in that lot?'

The girl rummaged through the pile, the gold chain, watches, wallets, smartphones. The girl was thorough. She found a small key in one of the wallets. Nicola unlocked the cuff. She dropped the limp arm, already getting cold. The briefcase was heavy, very heavy. He had been a strong man.

Nicola carried the briefcase over to the pile of wallets and tried the cuff key in the lock. It didn't work.

'Find a bag or pillowcase we can put all this other stuff in,' Nicola said. The girl came back with an old mail sack. Nicola threw everything in it. Except any cash she found in the wallets.

Blood was smeared over wallets and smart phones. Nicola became aware of the smell of blood iron in the air and was starting to taste it. It became sickly and sweet with hints of acetone. One eye still groaned.

'Let's get out of here,' Nicola said.

The girl followed. They threw everything in the back of the Chevy and slid the cover over. The girl still had the .38 stub nose. Nicola had the .357. She took the gun off the girl and put both guns in the glove compartment. There were a couple of boxes of .357 ammo in there. Nicola looked at the light aircraft and thought about it, she shuddered and decided to take the pickup. They closed the doors and floored it, covering the old Dodge Ram in dust. Nicola stopped at the junction with the blacktop road. She craned her head to see if the boy was there, but he had gone. Nicola checked the fuel gauge, just over three quarters. The girl was silent, staring wide eyed. Nicola grabbed her hand, squeezed it gently and then let go of it and put the truck in drive. She drove away from the town.

Nicola shot occasional glances at the girl. She had been silent for over an hour. They crossed the county border and another hour later they arrived at the outskirts of a bigger town. They pulled into an open area with a cluster of buildings, a gas station, convenience store, agricultural machinery dealers. Nicola pulled into the gas station and got out. She filled up the tank. Had a quick look around the pickup and made sure the sliding cover over the back was locked. The vehicle was covered in dust. The licence plates completely obscured. She opened the passenger door. The girl had been sleeping.

'You OK?' Nicola said. She gripped the girl's hand. The girl nodded.

'I'm Nicola.'

'I'm Layka.'

'Pleased to meet you Layka. – Do you want anything?'

'Just some water.'

Nicola went into the store, got some water and snacks and approached the counter. A friendly teenage girl with braces served her.

'You have FedEx or UPS?' Nicola said.

'They have UPS in the store across the way,' she said.

Nicola thanked her and went back to the pickup. The door was open. Layka had gone.

Nicola put the drinks and snacks on the passenger seat. She checked the back of the pickup. The sliding cover was still over the back and still locked. She unlocked it and checked. The briefcase and the bag were still there. Nicola cast her eyes around. She couldn't waste anymore time. She checked through the bag. Checked all the smartphones, all of them were locked, she didn't have the time to try and hack into them. She went through the wallets to double check for another key to the briefcase. She took out her binoculars and night vision goggles and put them on the back seat. She looked up again to see if she could see Layka. Nicola didn't have time to deal with her. She wished her all the best. Nicola had done all she could.

She took the bag and bunched it up. Slid over the cover and locked it. She shut the door and locked the truck and walked over to the store.

'Do you have a strong box I can send this in?' she said.

A dour man in his sixties said nothing and pointed to a rack with various UPS boxes. She took one, made it up and sealed the sack into it.

She went to the counter.

'Can I borrow a pen?' she said.

'I just need the address. I'll print the label,' he said.

'It's in France,' she said.

'That's no problem.'

Nicola gave him an address in the South West of Paris.

'What name?' he said.

'Phillippe.'

'And?'

'Just Phillippe.' She spelt it out to him.

'How quick do you want it there?'

'Fast as possible.'

He turned and looked at the clock.

'You're lucky, the pickup's late, it should arrive tomorrow.'

'Good,' she said and paid him cash.

Nicola walked back to the truck. Layka stood beside it.

'I wanted some air,' Layka said. Nicola hugged her tight.

*   *   *

'Where are your parents?'

'Gone,' Layka said.

'Gone?'

'Gone. Months ago.'

'Were you living in that house alone?'

'Yes, and hiding there.'

'Why did those men turn up?'

'They saw me buying stuff in town, they followed me one day, but I thought I shook 'em off.'

'When did they follow you back from town?'

'About a couple of weeks.'

'I guess it was just a process of elimination,' Nicola said.

'I guess.'

Layka started crying. Nicola held her hand. She decided to stop asking questions and concentrated on the dead straight road.

9

Sheriff's Deputy Novak drove the boy back to the old airfield.

'You OK driving back Bob?' she said. The boy was still woozy and had walked a good couple of miles before getting picked up by Novak.

'I'm OK,' he said, rubbing the back of his neck. He didn't look good, but there was no one else to drive his truck back. If it was still there.

They pulled up the track to the airfield, driving steadily. The boy was afraid. This was forbidden territory, everyone knew that.

When they got to the building, Bob was relieved to see his truck. The door to the building was open. It moved in the wind. Deputy Novak sensed something and readied her hand on her pistol before even getting out of the pickup.

'See if your truck's OK and wait for me out here,' she said. Bob went over to the Dodge.

Novak readied her pistol and crept towards the door. She gasped so loud that Bob came to see. He threw up in the doorway. Novak looked at him.

'Wait outside,' she said. Bob sat down hard on the dirt, leaning against the outside wall near the door. He gagged and then trembled.

Novak stepped around the congealing blood the best she could. She checked every room and found the naked bound man. She could see he'd been tortured. She looked in the back room, seeing the empty tripod, then she went through the pockets of Doug's corpse, then the others and realised their ID and phones were gone. She felt the blood drain from her face. Her fingertips tingled.

'Get in here Bob,' she shouted, her voice almost failing.

'I don't want to—I can't,' he shouted back from outside.

'You need to get in here Bob.'

'I can't.'

Novak went outside and pointed her pistol at Bob. His jaw fell open, words couldn't come. The confusion overwhelmed him.

'Get inside,' she said.

Bob got to his feet and raised his hands. He shook as he entered the building. Novak followed behind and shot him in the back of the head.

* * *

Nicola had taken a long route round to the north of the town. Layka woke up and recognised the area, she almost jumped out of her seat, gripping the door handle and tugging at her seatbelt.

'You've brought us back?' Layka said, almost shouting, rasping, high pitched. Jerking her head left and right to see if it was true.

'I have something I need to do.'

'We can't come back here, they'll kill us, turn back.'

Nicola pulled the car over. She shut down the engine. The silence was almost unbearable. The prairie, like a gold-brown ocean frozen in time and vanishing to every horizon. Whisps of clouds tried to make tornadoes in the distance. Nicola unfastened her seatbelt and turned to the girl.

'What happened to your parents?' Nicola said. The girl shuddered. Nicola held her hand.

'They came in the night.'

'Who?'

'Those men back there.'

'How did you get away?'

Layka started to cry. Nicola waited. Eventually the girl began to speak.

'I ran,' she said and she couldn't say anymore.

'They've gone now,' Nicola said.

Layka wept harder. Nicola offered her a bottle of water. She took it and began to drink.

'I will keep you safe,' Nicola said.

Layka wiped her face with the back of her hand.

'Let's get some air,' Nicola said and she got out, walked round and opened the passenger door.

Layka got out. Nicola took a look at her head. Blood had matted into her hair.

'Your head OK? They hit you hard?' Nicola said.

'Not that hard, I faked being unconscious.'

Nicola hugged her and Layka hugged her back.

'I'll make sure you are OK, I promise,' Nicola said.

Dusk suddenly came upon them, the light faded. They walked a little way into the grass. The wind began to pick up and with it a hint of the past winter. Layka wrapped her arms around herself and shivered. She looked across the landscape.

'It doesn't look like much to some people, but I love it,' Layka said.

'Come on,' Nicola said and led her back to the pickup. 'I have a place nearby.'

They took the pickup down a thin track and then across the prairie. The truck bumped and rocked, they tossed about and Nicola had to lean forward and hold tight the wheel. They came to a small dry creek, cut deep and out of view that hid the truck below the line of the horizon. Nicola then drove the Chevy down the steep bank, crabbing over loose ground. Feeling as if the truck would roll over, Layka gripped the sides of her seat. They got to the almost flat bottom of the dry creek and Nicola shut down the engine.

Layka thought she knew every inch of this country, but she never knew this place existed. It looked as if water hadn't flowed along it in a thousand years. It was out of the wind. Dead still and calm, silent and felt safe. They got out. Layka cast her eyes around. It was almost like being inside a building or cave, the air was so still.

'Follow me,' Nicola said, and they walked a little way up the dry creek, turning to the right. There was an old kiln nestled in the bank, Nicola had stretched a tarp over the top and weighed it down with turf. It had a thick sheet of hessian over the entrance, Layka pulled it back. The inside was a cone shape, beehive-like, blackened wall built of rock. There were the remains of a fire, a stack of firewood, two duffle bags hanging up from a piece of iron driven into the wall and nothing else. Suddenly a shaft of light came through the very top of the roof, some dirt fell on the hearth. Layka looked up to see the silhouette of Nicola's face look down, then go. A few seconds later Nicola pulled back the door cover.

'Let's build a fire,' Nicola said.

Layka smiled. Nicola saw in her a burst of energy, almost happiness and Nicola unhooked the bags and looked in them as Layka built the fire.

Nicola started the fire with a flint and knife and took some dried food out of a bag. She closed the bags and arranged them as seats. The fire began to take. Layka stared into the flames and her eyes reflected the fire. Nicola looked at her. She seemed calm, or at least able to cope with her thoughts and memories. Outside it was now night. Nicola passed her a piece of jerky.

'How did you find this place?' Layka said.

'From above, air photos, satellite.'

The flames began to dance casting shadows. Layka looked around.

'How long have you stayed in here?' Layka said.

'I spent the whole winter here.'

'What are you doing here? Why?'

'I think we want the same thing,' Nicola said. Layka said nothing. 'You need to tell me everything you know about the factory.'

Layka looked into Nicola's eyes and gave a single nod.

IO

By the time Novak drove away from the airfield, the plane, the truck and the building were ablaze. Black plumes of burning kerosine and other things rose high in the air. Then the wind came and blew the smoke flat and low. It intensified the heat. If anyone saw it, they would ignore it. Everyone knew to put their curiosity aside when it came to goings on at the old airfield. By the morning it would all be black smoulder.

Novak woke next day after a sound sleep but with one thing left that nagged at her. She wrapped her big frame up in her uniform and took a drive to the hospital. She didn't stop for breakfast.

The drive to the main town took two hours. Out of her jurisdiction. She arrived at the hospital before visiting time, but the nurse at the desk smiled and said it would be OK. She pointed Novak in the direction of a private room. Novak gently opened the door.

Rick slept. He lay on his back filling the expanse of the bed. He had an oxygen mask on. An IV bag hung up on a frame feeding saline into his arm. Novak hovered over him and looked at his face for a few seconds. She

189

then leant back and took a small, hard box out of her pocket. She opened the box. In it was a small syringe. She held it up to the light, cleared any bubbles and then injected it into the injection port of the IV bag. She put the syringe back in the small box and put it back in her pocket.

Novak took a good look at Rick's face again and went over to the door to listen for footsteps. She then took the bag off the frame, squeezed the injection port and rocked the bag back and forth. She then hung it back on the frame. She opened the cupboard by his bed and found his smartphone. She took another good look at Rick and left the room and walked back to the reception.

'He's out of it,' Novak said to the nurse. 'I'll come back a little later, do you have a cafeteria?'

* * *

Nicola and Layka woke at dawn. The night was comfortable. They ate some of the dried food quickly and drank from some bottled water. They went to the pickup, slid open the back and dragged near the briefcase. Layka saw something else in the back and her eyes lit up. The wire cutters. She picked them up with reverence and disbelief. Nicola observed her.

'Why are they so important to you?' Nicola said.

'They're all I have left of Dad.'

Layka put the cutters into her pocket. Nicola pulled the tailgate down and dragged the briefcase onto it. She looked at the lock.

'Let's see if there's any tools,' Nicola said and they scoured the cab of the pickup. They couldn't find anything of use, so Nicola picked up a rock.

'Wait!' Layka said. 'What if it's a bomb or something?'

'I don't think it's a bomb.'

Nicola repeatedly smashed at the lock. Layka hid behind the pickup. The front of the case stoved in and eventually the lock gave. Inside was a disappointment. Four old lead sash weights.

'You can come out now,' Nicola said. Layka peeked over the back of the pickup.

'What are they?' Layka said.

'Junk – I guess you can't trust criminals. Come on, let's go.' Nicola tossed the case and closed up the back of the truck. They got in, started the engine and drove further along the creek until they found a way up.

'I'm not sure about this,' Layka said.

'I spent the whole winter there, under twenty-five feet of snow, just so I could be here with no one knowing. I would have done what I needed to do, and no one would have seen me, then you came along. I don't blame you Layka, we want the same thing. If we don't do it now, it won't ever get done. They'll win.'

Layka said nothing. She felt she had said too much the night before. They rocked and bobbed over the prairie grass and got to the track.

* * *

Novak slid the tray in the rack. She had eaten enough to feed two people. She went back to the hospital reception and asked if she could go back in and see Rick. It was still too early for visitors, but she let the Deputy go back to the room.

Rick was awake. He lay flat, the oxygen mask still on. His breathing was labouring a little, but for now he was OK.

'You OK sport?' Novak said.

Rick lowered the mask.

'Been better,' he said. His words labouring. 'But they think I'll be OK.'

'Nothing broken then?' Novak said.

'Just real bad bruising, I'll be fine, how's the others?'

'They're OK, missing you though.' Novak smiled.

'You get that bitch?'

'Not yet,' Novak said.

'You will, right?'

'I'll get her Rick, you know I take care of you boys, as long as you don't keep anything from me, I'll keep you tight.'

Novak stared hard at Rick, she loomed over him, her face framed by sagging cheeks. His face flushed.

'You need to tell me anything Rick?'

Rick gulped and wheezed. He took a few slugs of oxygen from the mask. It hissed like a snake. That told Novak all she needed to know.

'Goodbye sport,' she said and she walked out of the room.

II

Nicola drove to the old burnt house. It smouldered, flat charred remnants crackled, and in a couple of years, barely a trace would be left. An outbuilding half-remained and she edged the truck under it. Nicola took the .357 and Layka the .38 and they got out of the truck.

'Who lived here?' Nicola said.

'Some old guy, died a couple of years ago.' Layka had a tear in her eye, it had been her home, her hiding place.

Heat still soaked out of the ground and a mix of smells, of natural and man-made objects permeated. Nicola made sure the truck was out of sight, parked back in the shadows of the old, broken outbuilding.

'Let's go,' Nicola said and Layka gulped. Her young eyes showed their true age, stripped momentarily from adult pain. Nicola held her hand and led her to the unmade track and towards the factory.

* * *

Novak drove fast. When she crossed back into the county, she drove faster. A faint column of smoke rose from the airfield, but she didn't look. She kept her eyes ahead and the tyres squealed as she took the turn to the factory. Under her breath she mumbled expletives, mostly ending with the word 'Idiots.'

She drove up to the loading doors and clicked a remote to open them. Two large doors opened out, foot-thick steel with giant shoot-bolts drawn back in them. She drove in and shut down the engine. No tours scheduled for today, the factory ran on autopilot. The robot arms in the viewing area were still. Novak checked the schedule on a screen. Things ran as they should. She shut the doors and they closed smooth and silent. Novak checked to see if anything showed up on the cameras. Nothing. So she decided to walk the rooms and corridors.

Most of the rooms and areas of the factory were empty. Set aside for future expansion. They acted as a buffer zone to the small central core. Novak wasn't too sure about the exact purpose of the factory.

Viewed from above, the outcrop of hills above the undulating prairie hinted to an event long ago. It left behind a geological anomaly. Something special. Something revered when first seen by people. Somewhat godlike, it sat in Earth sleeping. Its power, comprehended by few.

Novak opened the door to the central area. The only door embossed with the company logo. Mon AG, part of Klober Industries Inc. The door opened to a viewing platform, sealed off. A series of protocols, protective clothing and airlocks were between Novak and the sight before her. She watched and went no further. It frightened her. A large robot arm gently agitated and sucked up rock and dirt surrounding it. A large, glassy, amber object. Something about it made Novak shudder. She left and closed the door.

Novak went to another room, still in the core of the factory. In this room, dozens of small CNC machines worked on fragments of the large object in the room nearby. There were other rooms like this, each with dozens of machines. Above, a pipe rattled with the spoil excavated from around the object. It went to a large hopper to be loaded onto trucks when necessary. Everything seemed to be in order. But it wasn't.

At the other end of the building a small hatch had been breached. Nicola hadn't discovered it, but Layka had. Nicola wasn't sure if she would be able to fit through it. The hatch was a mistake. An outlet for pipes and cables that were never installed. A misreading of the plans by the contractor and covered up to avoid repercussions. Layka went first. Nicola passed the .357 to her and squeezed through. It was tight, Nicola felt as if she was being swallowed. Spare .357 rounds pushed into her upper thighs through her pockets. But she got through, though she was sore and bruised. They were in a large duct, almost big enough for Nicola to stand in. Footprints were ahead in the duct, Layka's.

Layka passed the .357 to Nicola and she tucked it in her waist. Neither spoke, light came in from the entrance and reflected, so they could see enough.

An intruder alert registered on a smartphone, but the phone sat in a box travelling the last mile to Paris. Phones couldn't work in the factory. Novak felt uneasy and was torn between leaving and staying.

Layka and Nicola made their way through the ducts and came into a room intended to house machinery. It was empty, with traces of construction dust. Layka's footprints from before were in the dust. The light was dim, but enough to see the outline of the girl and the woman. When they opened the door, the pale, permanent light in the corridor almost blinded them.

'This way,' Layka whispered.

Layka took the lead, both of them placed their steps with great care. Layka's shoe squeaked and Nicola's heart missed a beat. Nicola wanted to hold back, go slow, but Layka rushed ahead. She turned right at the end of the corridor out of sight. Nicola angered, she broke into a jog. She rounded the corner and jolted to a stop, her arms waving to keep her balance.

Novak had her hand clasped around Layka's mouth and she pointed a gun to her head.

12

Cyril sat in the reception of the old motel. He was stubborn. The corporation had bought the town, they had bought the whole county. They had paid him twice the market value of the old Motel, but he insisted on staying there, like he always had. He even convinced them to pay him a salary. The town meeting went his way, they were fond of him, they talked the corporation into letting him have his way. The lawyer made a phone call, nodded to the assembled town, packed up his briefcase and couldn't get out of town quick enough. The town had a new, duly elected Sheriff. But he operated in absentia. And he was the only candidate put forward for election. All the real business was dealt with by the deputy, Novak.

Cyril, at first, thought he had won. He thought his old-time morals would see him through, keep him straight. But he kept being drawn deeper, little by little.

Something broke in Cyril's mind when he told Nicola a junkie had died in the motel room. The lie burnt into his soul. Just two years ago, he wouldn't lie, couldn't.

He made his way carefully up the rotting metal staircase and went into the room with the police tape. He ripped the flapping, broken tape away, balled it up and tossed it into the room. He got down awkwardly on his knees by the bed and looked under it. He ran his hands around and smiled. The earring was gone. It had been there so long, he feared it wouldn't be found. It was a little thing, almost hopeless, but it was something. He was glad he had done something. Something told him that Nicola was the right one to find it.

It was a long time since Cyril had felt this kind of lightness and he let himself daydream and think of the old times and the people who had gone. He looked out from the balcony and yawned, and he stepped onto the staircase, thinking it was 1962, and the staircase crumbled.

Cyril didn't mind dying, he felt quite calm when it came.

13

Novak said nothing. She smiled. Layka's eyes stared wide at Nicola. Novak's meaty hand clasped just below them. Her other hand wrapped the pistol, pressed into the girl's head.

'You're going to die Novak, let her go,' Nicola said. Novak grinned, sweat shone on her face.

'How did you get in here?' Novak said. She pressed the muzzle harder into Layka's head and the girl let out a muffled cry. Her eyes now wet.

'Let her go and I'll show you,' Nicola said.

'Take out the gun and put it on the ground,' Novak said. Nicola hesitated, Novak pushed the gun harder into Layka's skull. Nicola removed the .357 from her belt and crouched down, laying it on the ground. She glanced towards Layka and saw the .38 still tucked in her waist. It had ridden down, only a hint of the grip visible. Nicola shot a fast glance at it and looked deep into Layka's eyes.

'It's gonna be fine,' she said. Layka's eyes showed fear. Nicola hoped she got the hint. Layka's arms hung by her sides. She brushed her hand over the gun. Nicola smiled at her and she stood back up and raised her hands.

'Who are you really Novak?' Nicola said.

Novak said nothing, she nodded towards where they had come from and moved forward. Novak kicked the .357 out of the way. Nicola backed away. She turned the corner, Novak quickened her pace, almost dragging Layka. Layka was too afraid to go for the pistol. It would be too awkward.

Nicola pressed tight against the wall and then leapt at Novak as she rounded the corner, driving her fist into Novak's jaw. Novak was stunned, but didn't go down, she tightened her grip on Layka. Layka bit hard at Novak's hand. Nicola got behind Novak and got her left arm around her neck and got Novak into a sleeper hold, but Novak still gripped Layka. Blood flowed from Novak's hand and smeared on Layka's face.

Novak was like a bull, hot stiff muscle. Her body armour rasped into Nicola's skin. She slammed Nicola into the wall, lifting her off her feet, still holding on to Layka and flinging her around. Nicola tightened her hold, Novak slammed her into the wall twice more and then let go of Layka and clawed at Nicola's arm.

Novak buckled at the knees and went down. Nicola tightened a little more. Layka fumbled and got hold of the .38. She pulled the hammer back.

'No!' Nicola shouted. Layka looked confused. 'I want her alive. Novak succumbed, Nicola dropped her down, took out her cuffs and cuffed her hands behind her back. Novak had a second set of cuffs, bigger, so Nicola cuffed Novak's ankles, they just fit, they dug in and would hurt. Nicola checked her, found two smart phones, a small throwing knife strapped to her left calf, a door pass and nothing else.

With Novak trussed up, Nicola turned to Layka. She was sitting, crying, holding the pistol, the hammer back. Nicola took the .38 off Layka and sat down next to her. She put her arm around Layka.

'What if she had shot me?' Layka said.

'She wouldn't have.'

'How do you know?'

'She left the safety on her pistol.'

'Why didn't you just shoot her?'

'I need to talk to her.'

'But you wanted me to shoot her?'

'You're a smart girl, I'm glad you got the hint, but I reckoned on you missing and just spooking her.'

'What if I didn't miss?'

'Then we would have improvised.'

Novak groaned, Layka and Nicola looked at her. Novak got herself up enough to lean against the wall.

'You don't know what you're dealing with,' Novak said.

'I do,' Nicola said, 'but you need to fill in some details for me.' Novak spat on the floor and stared hard at Nicola.

'Or not,' Nicola said. 'You can stay silent, and stay here and burn with this building. I don't give a shit.'

Nicola held up the two smart phones.

'I'll send these to my friend too,' Nicola said.

Novak said nothing, but started to sweat. Nicola looked at her, waiting. Novak decided to speak.

'That was nothing to do with me,' she said.

'It's everything to do with you now Deputy Novak. I think your real bosses will be a little upset. I think leaving you to die here will be a mercy.'

Novak swallowed hard.

'But I don't understand exactly who your bosses are,' Nicola said. 'They should all be gone.'

'You can't get rid of them, they warned me about you, said you would be coming,' Novak said.

Nicola's heart sank. She tried not to show it. She feared the impossibility of destroying Klober's empire. She thought she had cut the head off the snake.

Nicola looked over to Layka. She sat there, looking forward, in a trance. She looked as though she hadn't heard anything, but then she spoke,

'Where did you dump my parents?'

'I left it to the bozos, kid,' Novak said. Her eyes cold and shark like. 'I tried to persuade your folks to stop protesting kid . . . everyone else listened.'

Layka walked past Novak and round the corner into the other corridor. She came back with the .357. She walked back to Novak and pulled back the hammer.

'Don't,' Nicola said. 'Killing her in cold blood will stay with you.'

Layka wept. She wiped her eyes with the back of her hand. She didn't acknowledge Nicola. Nicola stood up and moved slowly towards Layka. Layka pointed the gun at Nicola. Nicola held up her hands.

'Don't do it Layka, it will be unbearable—forever,' Nicola said.

Novak grinned, she tried to look calm, though sweat ran down her face.

'That face will always be there, etched right into you, you'll always see it,' Nicola said. The heavy gun trembled in Layka's hand.

Nicola approached her slowly and took the gun from her.

'You've been through enough,' Nicola said. Layka wept and held Nicola. Novak grinned. Nicola looked at the bulge near Novak's ankle and remembered the throwing knife. She had put it on the ground nearby. She picked it up.

'Not exactly standard issue for a deputy,' Nicola said.

Novak spat on the ground. Nicola knew she was too tough to break.

'You got sloppy, you're frightened,' Nicola said. 'And now I'm in here, I have no use for you.' Nicola held up the door pass. 'Your bosses were wiped out in Paris, who gives you orders?'

Novak smiled. 'Go ahead. You think they will forgive me for this?' she said.

'Go on along the corridor and don't look back Layka,' Nicola said.

'Who are you?' Novak said and these were her last words. Nicola looked to make sure Layka was far enough away, and she pushed the knife between the vertebrae of Novak's neck.

14

Nicola jogged to catch up with Layka.

'You OK?' she said to Layka. She didn't reply, Layka felt ashamed for pointing the gun at Nicola.

'Don't worry about it,' Nicola said and she gave Layka a comforting grip on the shoulder, Layka rested her hand on Nicola's.

'Know where we're going?' Nicola said. Layka nodded.

'This way,' Layka said. Nicola followed her lead.

They used Novak's door pass to enter a small control room. Several screens showed the excavation process. The screens were high-definition colour. The smoky amber glass reminded Nicola of the earring and she reached into her pocket and took it out.

Layka stared at the screens and shuddered, then she looked at Nicola and gasped. She clamped her hand to her mouth and sat on the floor. Nicola looked down at her.

'What?'

Layka couldn't speak. She hyperventilated. Nicola crouched down, put her hand on Layka's shoulder and said, 'What is it?' Layka held out her hand and reached for the earring. Nicola gave it to her. Layka wept hard. Nicola understood.

'It's your mother's isn't it?' Nicola said.

Layka clasped the earring in both hands and continued to weep.

'Let's do this for her,' Nicola said and she wiped Layka's eyes and used the moisture from her tears to wipe away Novak's blood.

'This place is sacred, special,' Layka said, 'I can't do it.' Her eyes welled up again.

'You know we must,' Nicola said.

'They fought so hard for this place,' Layka said.

'They fought hard to stop this factory,' Nicola said. 'We must do it.'

On the screens the robots worked meticulously. Scraping, excavating, mining. Small chips split from the glassy core. The small CNC machines shaping and carving. A quantum leap in Klober's technology. A new way of creating their core product, unimaginable, genius. Indestructible switches, impervious to radiation, heat, electrical interference. Depending on the shape of the scratch made on them, they would only work at a given electromagnetic frequency. Used to destroy and create and to dominate. Klober's technology would hold dominion over the world and eventually beyond.

Nicola hoped there was no other place like this. At least not one that could be found.

'Are we going to save the world?' Layka said.

'No,' Nicola said.

'So why do you want to do this?'

Nicola traced her fingers over a small aluminium plate, riveted to the console. It said *Klober Inc.*

'I want to destroy everything to do with that name,' Nicola said.

'Why?'

Nicola said nothing. She thought about how Klober had waved his genius under her nose, desperate for someone to recognise his greatness. She was angry that she had missed so much of what he tried to imply. He had left her clues that only now she was able to see. She hated him. He wouldn't die from her mind or thoughts. She couldn't be free of him until everything he had influenced had been destroyed and she knew the irony of that.

Nicola hoped she was right about the means to destroy this place, or rather that she hadn't been tricked. There was only one way to ensure reliable power for the factory. Fuel would be hard to deliver in the harsh North Western winters. The factory could not stop. So the answer came from Klober's defence arm, or rather from one of the companies it controlled. As far as the authorities, or anyone who should have cared was concerned, the factory was powered by hydrogen, kickstarted by the solar panels and an aquifer that collected water from spring thawed snow. Stored hydrogen then powered the plant through the winter and the night.

But it didn't. There was no way the power demands of the place could be met with green technology. Nicola looked at Layka, she held the earing and stared at it. The earing was made from a fragment of the precious ore, but it was rarer, stable, or it was stable because of its shape and size. Crafted by a genius who knew its secrets.

If the mass of the deposit was exposed to the right mix of light or electromagnetic energy, it would destroy itself. Nicola looked again at the console and searched through the protocol she had seared into her memory. She shut down the nuclear reactor that powered the place and she waited. Nothing. The protocol was wrong. Residual power kept the machines working. She expected that, but something should have happened.

Rage began to fill Nicola. She clenched her fists. Layka watched her, silent. Nicola hung her head, her blonde hair hid her face, falling lank.

'We're not meant to be doing this. It's stopping us,' Layka said.

'Fuck him,' Nicola said and she thumped the name-plate with *Klober Inc* written on it. The console shuddered. Nicola's fist rested in a shallow dent. Layka looked at her. Scared. Amazed at her strength. Nicola lifted her fist and looked at the dent and she wondered at her bursts of strength. She didn't know where they came from, why they weren't always there when she needed them.

'Look,' Layka said. Nicola looked at her.

'What?'

Layka pointed at the screens. The machines had stopped moving. Only something was changing. Numbers in the corner of one of the screens began to rise like milliseconds on a stopwatch. Above the numbers were the letters pT.

A crack formed on the glassy ore and the crane above it jolted and fractured. The building began to groan, cracks now radiated over the ore and pieces fell away. Nicola grabbed Layka's hand and they ran back the way they had come. Layka glanced at Novak's corpse. Less blood than expected. The building began to scream as reinforcing bars in concrete stretched and the building felt as if it began to move. Spider cracks widened and the floor began to warp. Nicola tripped and tumbled forward, dragging Layka with her. It was difficult to get back up, like being in an earthquake.

They got to the room and then to the ducting. Nicola almost threw Layka into the duct. She crawled in after her.

The ducting twisted and the dim light vanished.

'Layka!'

Dirt began to rattle into the tightening duct. Layka didn't reply.

15

A fissure zigzagged along the ground and then more, radiating from the isolated nest of hills above the prairie. The building juddered. It began to sink in small bursts. The scale of the deposit, so vast, the factory and the hills sat upon it. A lifetime's worth of the precious resource, now being destroyed by the failure of a shield. The Montana earth and rock made the perfect cloak, protecting the deposit for millennia, perhaps longer. Now it would vibrate itself to dust and gas.

Nicola's eyes fixed shut, pressed against dirt. It choked her, coated her dry tongue. Her hand reached forward, gripped by rocks and dirt and twisted metal. Her heart beat fast, she thought of Layka. Her forward hand gripped at the rocks and dirt and she dragged herself, little by little. She wondered how she was breathing. She crawled in the black abyss and was sure that she had died. But she wanted to go on, fight through the fog and confusion, test if this really was death.

She felt air on her hand and then another hand gripped hers and then through the dirt in her eyes she saw daylight. She forced herself forwards and she saw the outline of Layka. The factory and the hills around were now a dusty crater. The ground rumbled and loose rocks and fallen trees slid into the middle of the crater and began to sink.

The girl and woman got to the top and onto the prairie and they dusted themselves down the best they could. They had to walk far before the radiating fissures were narrow enough to cross. Nicola held Layka's hand, neither felt the need to speak. They walked a great distance and as dusk fell, they got to the edge of a remote property with an old house far away on a hill. An old man with long grey hair opened the distant door. Layka handed Nicola the two phones taken from Novak and Nicola smiled.

'How can I look him in the face? I've killed a god,' Layka said.

'No you haven't. We've killed a devil.'

Layka began to walk to the house. Nicola stood still.

'How would you have gotten in there without me?' Layka said.

'I would have dyed my hair and gone on a guided tour.'

Layka smiled and ran back to Nicola, they hugged. Both cried. Layka walked back towards the house.

'Layka!' Nicola said.

'Yes?'

'You might want to spread the word that there is a damaged nuclear reactor under there.'

16

Nicola stopped at the first FedEx store she could find. She put the phones she had taken from Novak in a box and wrote a note:

Phillippe,
  A PS to the last package. Send to your friends in Lyon.
  The head is still on the snake.
  Watch yourself.
  Sorry. X
  N